The Boy of Her Choice

Mike did not envy her younger sister Pat. She did not want a bracelet which represented the concerted adoration of ten boys. She wanted one boy, one intense and admiring boy, who preferred her above all other girls.

And she knew the boy she wanted. She had seen him several times when she had gone to the boys' basketball games. He was captain of the team. People said he was also a champion skier. Mike had watched him from a distance, admiring him, wishing she could know him.

Mike was also thinking about what she would ever do or say if she accidentally ran into him, when suddenly, confronting her, was the boy of her choice . . .

MY SISTER MIKE

Amelia Elizabeth Walden

A BERKLEY HIGHLAND BOOK
published by
BERKLEY PUBLISHING CORPORATION

Published by arrangement with
McGraw-Hill Book Company, Inc.

SBN-425-03915-3

BERKLEY HIGHLAND BOOKS are published by
Berkley Publishing Corporation
200 Madison Avenue, New York, N.Y. 10016

Berkley Highland Books ® TM 758,135

Printed in the United States of America

BERKLEY HIGHLAND EDITION, MARCH, 1963

ONE

MIKE PATTERSON sat on the bench next to Miss Yates, the Westbrook coach. She hunched over, her hands dangling in front of her, her eyes restlessly watching the clock and scoreboard.

The game was in the bag. It was just a matter of sitting it out until the buzzer sounded. The scoreboard told the story: Brighthaven, 12; Visitors, 36. The visitors were Westbrook. Mike smiled broadly as she watched the play. Miss Yates had sent in her second team, giving the greenhorns a chance to get the feel of a varsity game. Even with Westbrook's second team in there, Brighthaven was having a hard time.

It was a bad year for Brighthaven. They had lost most of their good players with the June graduation. Sometimes a brand-new team was an improvement, if the new team consisted of girls who were natural basketball players. But these new Brighthaven players were real greenhorns, much worse than Westbrook's second team.

Most of them had not even learned how to pass. Mike doubted if they had ever heard of a hook shot, a controlled tap, a dummy play, a follow-in, a stride stop. She looked them over, shaking her head. It wasn't the Brighthaven coach's fault either. Mrs. Crawford knew her stuff. These young kids just didn't have what it takes.

It's going to be a tough year for Brighthaven, Mike thought. And that makes us Westbrookers feel real bad.

Sarcasm was not her forte, because by nature she liked people. She didn't enjoy watching anyone have a hard time. But feeling sorry for Brighthaven would be treason to Westbrook since the schools were traditional enemies. When they faced each other, no matter what the sport, they played for blood. If the tables had been turned,

Brighthaven would have been gloating over Westbrook —with a show of sportsmanship, but gloating just the same.

Her eyes following the play, Mike saw one of Westbrook's substitute forwards come down too hard and turn her ankle. Mike saw it quickly, with her athlete's sixth sense, even before the referee blew the whistle. There were excited exclamations back of her as she jumped from the bench and ran over to where they were helping the injured girl off the floor. It was Lynn Craig, a freshman to whom Mike had taken a liking. Lynn played good basketball. As they led her over to a bench and both coaches bent over her, she smiled gamely.

Miss Yates turned to Mike who had followed them. "Ready to go in again?" she asked. Mike had come out of the game only a minute or so before.

Mike nodded and running over to the scorer's table said crisply, "Patterson going in for Craig." As she joined the other forwards, she called her instructions. "Feed them to me as fast as you can."

The referee's whistle blew. Mike got the ball and tapped it into Westbrook territory. The two substitute forwards kept the ball and passed it to Mike. She played way out in center court, hurling a hook shot clean into the basket. It was grandstand playing and she knew it, but she figured she was entitled to it. This was her moment. She did not get many of them off the basketball court. This was the only place she could shine. So she took that moment, hooking them in for all she was worth.

Westbrook's score zoomed up. Thirty-eight. Forty. Forty-one on a free throw. Forty-three. Forty-five. Forty-six on another free throw. Brighthaven was tossing off fouls right and left. Forty-eight. Fifty.

The final buzzer rasped into the game. There was a flurry of activity from the stands as coats were hastily shrugged on, overshoes and boots yanked into place, scarves tied over heads. The small crowd milled out, climbing over each other, jumping down to the floor and racing for the exits.

The game was over. The cheering had already faded into oblivion and Mike Patterson, the great Mike Patterson who could hurl a hook shot from center floor clean into the basket, was tucked away in mothballs until the next game.

She linked arms with the other girls on her team as they cheered Brighthaven. At its side of the court, the Brighthaven team was cheering Westbrook. This final cheer always tickled Mike. It was such an empty gesture where these two schools were concerned.

The cheer over, a few of her teammates called, "Nice going, Mike. You played a terrific game." She waved off the compliments in good-natured appreciation.

Mike noticed that Emma Gaudet did not join in the congratulations. To say that Emma worried Mike would be putting it mildly. Emma who was Westbrook's best guard was also Mike's gadfly. Last year she had been difficult enough, with her cocky manner and sharp tongue, but now that they were seniors Emma spelled real trouble for Mike. Especially since Mike had been elected acting captain of the Westbrook team while the real captain was hospitalized for two months.

For the life of her, Mike could not put her finger on the cause of the strife between Emma and her. Emma never brought their conflict into the open. Most of her attacks on Mike were addressed to others rather than to Mike. She was past master at the art of subtle, squelching remarks that cut across Mike's ego as if she had been struck with a lash.

This cattiness of Emma's overwhelmed Mike. She just didn't know how to handle it. Brought up in a family where the straightforward approach was used in every situation, she felt paralyzed and numbed by Emma's indirect accusations.

One of Emma's favorite tricks was to be sure Mike was within earshot, then comment *sotto voce* to a friend, "Two-four-six-eight. Who don't we appreciate? P-a-t-t-e-r-s-o-n." It was Emma who had given Mike the inglorious nickname of "My Sister Mike," alluding to the fact that Mike was the less popular sister of one of the school's reigning beauties, Pat Patterson. And it was Emma who had first uttered the snide remark, "There's an awful lot of Patterson in this school. Mike Patterson runs the basketball team and Pat Patterson runs the cheerleaders. Pretty soon the whole Patterson family will be running the town."

Perhaps the most devastating and effective of Emma's thrusts were against Mike's appearance. Emma Gaudet had a repertory of insults directed toward Mike's lanky frame, her plain features, her drab hair, her lack of glamour.

"My Sister Mike," she would say in summary, "is a plain Jane. If she ever gets a steady boy friend, we'll declare a school holiday."

All in all, Emma was quite a problem. So Mike considered herself fortunate that Emma had only refrained from joining in the congratulations this afternoon.

On the way out of the gym, Mike found Lynn Craig waiting near the door that opened to the parking lot. She was leaning back against a radiator to take the weight off her right foot.

"How's it going?" Mike asked.

"It's all right," Lynn replied.

Mike examined the ankle. "When I saw you come down on it, I was afraid you'd sprained it for sure." She smiled up at Lynn. "You played a good game, but you don't have to try so hard." She nodded toward the ankle. "Things like this happen when we get too eager. Got a lift home, Lynn?"

"My mother's coming for me."

Mike nodded. "I was going to say I'd drive you myself."

Mike walked on. The locker rooms were noisy and steamy from a dozen showers. She took hers in a leisurely way. There was no reason to hurry. She had to pick up her sister Pat at Westbrook High where Pat was rehearsing for a play. Pat wouldn't be ready until six o'clock and it was just a little after five.

The girls of the team who were going back to nearby Westbrook on the special bus were in a hurry, shouting to each other to get a move on. Snatches of the talk reached Mike's ears above the noise of the showers.

"Where's my algebra book . . . ? I've lost Clint's fraternity pin. He'll crown me. Oh, here it is. . . . Hey, that's my coat. Here's yours. Wish you wouldn't buy your clothes in Carlson's Department Store too." A wave of laughter. Then, "Mike sure played a wonderful game today. . . . That's nothing, she always does. . . . She's tops. Plays with her head. Nobody can land a hook shot the way Mike can. Well, we all have to be good at something, I guess. . . . Yeah, that's right. We all have to be good at something."

Mike let the last words roll through her mind, slowly. She repeated them painstakingly. *We all have to be good at something.* Without intending it, the unidentified speaker had summed up Mike's character in a nutshell. She had, in fact, summed up Mike's entire life.

It had begun years ago, but she still remembered the exact time and the place. It was back in grade school—the fifth grade in old Center School. She remembered the day. She saw herself, a tall, skinny kid sauntering into the makeshift gym, a barren place, small, with uneven floor boards and a sliding partition that transformed it during the morning hours into two classrooms.

It was after school on a bleak December day just before Christmas. She was on her way down to buy presents for the family that afternoon when she heard shouting in the gym and, frankly curious, had poked her head in to see what was going on.

Some seventh-grade girls were playing and one of them overshot the mark and the ball lunged at Mike. Instinctively she put up her hands and the ball hit them. It was the first time she had ever held a basketball in her hands. She could feel the sting right now, this very moment, the smarting pain of that first time a basketball had hit her hands. She could even feel, in retrospect, the leather casing. She could still recall what the smell of that first basketball had been, the strong, pungent smell of leather in her nostrils.

She had stood there a moment, undecided, wondering if she should bounce the ball away from her or toss it to the older girls. One of them had cried out, "Shoot, Mike! See if you can make a basket." The girl pointed toward

9

the metal rim from which hung the torn and frayed knotted rope that answered for a basket in old Center School.

Mike had remained right where she was—she had been that ignorant!—and hurled the ball at the rim of the basket. It teetered a moment, then fell in.

The older girls had let out a howl. "Beginner's luck!" they roared. "Bet she couldn't do it again."

But she had. Mike had gone into their game and made basket after basket. Once in a while she missed, but not often. The girls were astonished. They fussed over her and flattered her. They asked where she had learned how to shoot baskets like that. When she protested that this was the first time she had held a basketball, they exchanged significant glances. They said it was all right with them if she wanted to kid them along.

Mike marked life as having really begun for her that December day. It was the first time in her life anyone had taken special notice of her. Until then she had always been Mike Patterson, one of the Patterson sisters, you know, those two girls with names that are so easy to get mixed up. Mike and Pat. The sisters, however, are very different. Pat is adorable. She's lovely to look at. Such charming manners and such a talented child. A born leader, too. She just seems to stand out. One of the most popular girls in her class. Everyone seems to revolve around Pat.

Mike? Well, Mike's the older one, you know. She's a little on the independent side. A lone wolf. Yes, she has some friends but it's her sister Pat whom everyone notices.

Basketball, for two months in the year, changed that. For two months—maybe a little longer—Mike had discovered that people would take notice of her. When she got out there on the gym floor, stood smack bang in the middle of the basketball court, and zoomed a hook shot clean into the basket, the spectators couldn't help but see it. The small crowd in the stands cheered. Her teammates, with the possible exception of Emma Gaudet, applauded her. Emma might disparagingly sneer, *"My Sister Mike* sure plays to the grandstand," but the rest of the team boomed her name in appreciation. They liked to

10

see Mike win for them. They clapped her on the back after each victory. They told her she was good, terrific, tops.

For about two months out of every year, Mike almost believed them.

We all have to be good at something.

The words tossed off so casually in the shower room stayed with her while she was getting dressed. They neither irritated nor pleased her, but they did amuse her. They amused her because of the accuracy with which they had struck their mark, like a well-aimed open shot hurling the ball straight through the basket.

She pulled on her cardigan, a dark brown with imitation pearl buttons and slipped on her single piece of jewelry, a bangle bracelet given her on her last birthday by her twin brothers who were juniors at Yale. She would have liked to own a charm bracelet, one of those noisy baubles with such things as hearts, miniature elephants, four-leaf clovers, telescopes, bells, and pixies dangling from a heavy gold chain. She would have liked to be presented with one of these charms on each "occasion," Christmas, Easter, her birthday, St. Valentine's Day, by some attractive boy.

Pat had such a bracelet. The original chain and first charm had been given her by one boy and the nine other charms which hung from it had been presented by nine different boys.

Mike did not envy her sister. She did not want a bracelet which represented the concerted adoration of ten boys. She wanted one boy, one intense and admiring boy, who preferred her above all other girls. One would be enough, providing that one was right.

She knew the boy she wanted. She was not sophisticated, as Pat was sophisticated. She had no background of experience with boys to bolster her in her selection, but with the same remarkable accuracy with which she had been able to toss her first basketball straight at its goal she made her choice of boy.

He belonged right here in Brighthaven. She had seen him several times when she had come over to boys' basketball games. He was captain of the team this year. Mike had seen him other places too, in the Greasy Spoon

11

where crowds of students from Brighthaven and West-brook gathered after games and skating parties. Once last winter when her brothers had taken her skiing on Rolling Giant, she had seen her boy there, taking the hardest slopes with ease. People said he was a champion skier, taught by some of the finest teachers in Europe. She had watched him from a distance, admiring him, wishing she could know him.

He was all that a man, in her limited knowledge of men, should be. He was tall, but not too tall, two inches above Mike's five-feet-eight. He was not handsome according to the standards set by girls like Pat who would not consider a boy unless he was good-looking enough to be eligible for movie stardom. He had a nice face, more gentle than arrogant, more patient than aggressive. Yet there was nothing weak about him. He was all man. Mike did not know how she knew this, but she did know it. He was the kind who would stand up to anything. No one would ever succeed in pushing him around.

Mike had been garnering information about her boy. He spoke four languages, Italian, French, German, English. He had traveled everywhere with his parents. His father was a professor and his mother played the piano. Not for her own amusement, the way Mike's twin brothers did, but for money. Ronnie, one of the twins, considered her the finest woman concert pianist in the East.

Mike thought about all this as she put on her coat and hat. She picked up her bag and slung it over her shoulder. Every time she came to Brighthaven, she dreamed what she would ever do or say if she accidentally ran into Jeff Parker.

Now she chuckled to herself as she walked toward the door of the locker room. The place was empty so she was safe in talking aloud to herself.

"Know what you'd do?" she said. "You'd bounce away from Jeff Parker like a 'hope shot' off the rim of a basket, that's what you'd do!"

She put her shoulder against the door and swung it open. There, confronting her, with two worry lines furrowing his brow was the boy of her choice.

12

TWO

MIKE DID not bounce away from Jeff Parker. She stood there, her eyes almost popping out of her head.

"Hello," she said, not knowing what else to say. "Are you looking for someone?"

Jeff Parker still looked worried as he said, "Yes, I'm looking for you. You are Mike Patterson, aren't you?" Mike nodded. "The last girl out said you were the only one left in there."

Mike had never been so close to the boy of her choice and she took the opportunity to appraise him. He sounded nice. His voice was appealing and he looked just as nice as he sounded. The large mouth was firmly chiseled, the brown of the eyes had a velvety texture, and the jaw, with a little more growing, would be all a man's jaw should be. She noted with satisfaction that standing this close he was definitely taller than she. So she had been right about that all-important factor.

"Sure you haven't lost something?" she asked. He answered "No-o-o," drawing the word out. She added, "You look bothered about something."

He brightened with an effort, forcing a smile, apparently not wanting to look bothered about anything.

He coughed, gulped, and squeezed the words out with apparent difficulty. "I'd like you to have dinner with me, Mike."

She rolled back on her heels, feeling behind her for something solid and almost losing her balance. Jeff caught her before she toppled and pulled her back.

"Dinner," he said firmly this time, "and a movie afterward."

Suddenly she realized the dreadful mistake he had

made. She laughed. "You've got me mixed up with my sister Pat. Lots of people who don't know us well get our names mixed. Mike and Pat." She spoke rapidly in nervous jerks. "I see what got you confused. Pat and I are usually here together. I play basketball. Pat is the cheerleader. Look, you'd better call her up. Our number is Cl 7-9605. Wait, I'll write it down for you." She rummaged in her disorderly bag for a pencil. As she was tearing a scrap of paper from her English notebook, Jeff stopped her.

"I haven't made any mistake. I want to take you to dinner, Mike. Not your sister Pat."

"You're sure?" She could feel her mouth drop open. She clamped it shut, making an embarrassing click.

"Yes, I'm positive."

Doubts crowded her. She couldn't understand why Jeff Parker would ask her for a date out of a clear sky. It seemed fantastic, much too good to be true. Yet the instinct within her that had made her choose this boy from all the boys she had ever known now rose to assert itself.

She squelched her doubts and asked, "When?"

"Tonight."

"Oh, no. I couldn't. That's too soon. I need time. Lots of time." She was talking nervously again.

"Tomorrow then." She liked the way he said that, with enough self-assertion to show a hidden strength.

"I guess maybe I could make it for then. What time?"

"Six-thirty. If it's all right with you, we'll go to Chimney Corner." She almost swooned. Chimney Corner was the most expensive place around, lying right between Brighthaven and Westbrook. She had expected Jeff to take her to the Kitchen Restaurant where most of the high-school boys took their dates.

He walked out of the building with her. She kept up a running conversation all the way. She had very little idea of what she was saying, but she felt excited and she simply had to let off steam. Jeff looked straight ahead, nodding from time to time. He hardly replied to her rapid-fire attempts at conversation.

Maybe he's just the quiet kind, she thought. "Can I give you a lift?" she asked. "My car—I mean my brothers' car is over there. Ronnie and Don—those are my twin brothers—are at Yale. They let Pat and me use the car while they're away." He was looking away from her. She felt he wasn't listening and he seemed strangely reserved, almost embarrassed. "How about a lift?" she asked again, eagerly.

"Thanks," he seemed to come suddenly awake, "but I've got my motorcycle right over there." He started away, then came back. "It's a sure date for tomorrow night then," he said, and his manner seemed almost business-like. "Six-thirty. You won't break it, will you, Mike?" His tone was apprehensive as he asked her that.

She told him the truth. "I've never broken a date with a boy in my life." He looked relieved and walked off toward his motorcycle. She stood watching him, frozen to the spot with admiration for Jeff and astonishment at her sudden good fortune. Jeff grabbed the handlebars of his motorcycle. With one deft kick on the pedal, he start-ed the engine, dropped into the saddle, and swung out on the road in a long graceful curve.

She sighed and shook herself from her trance. Getting into the car, she pulled out of the parking lot. Jeff waved her to come on. He followed her a short distance along the road to Westbrook, the chug-chug of his engine mak-ing a companionable sound. Then at a fork, he came alongside, blinked his lights in signal and turned off to-ward his home.

She waited until she could no longer see the fast-retreat-ing light of his motorcycle. Then she drove on.

Jeff Parker was a deep one, all right. He'd need some probing. There was a boy who couldn't be understood all in one piece.

Mike took the shore road to Westbrook because it was quicker. She'd have to hurry now or she'd be late. Pat was never a patient waiter. The Pattersons lived so far out that it was difficult to find anyone to give them lifts home. As she thought about her date with Jeff, she suddenly realized she hadn't told him where she lived. He hadn't even asked. Maybe she should turn back. She slowed down, then realized how foolish she would look running back after him. She could telephone him. No, that would be appearing too anxious. Let him find out where she lived.

The road was dark, with piles of snow banked along the shoulders to remind her that it was midwinter, but inside spring sang its song of renewal. The world and all life were new for Mike. If she had heard robins singing in the bare branches of the trees, she would not have been surprised.

I've got a date with Jeff Parker! her heart kept singing. Wait till Pat hears about it!

Pat and a boy were waiting inside the auditorium entrance. They came out, climbing into the front seat with Mike. The boy was Taylor Watkins. He talked about the "the-ah-tah." That was the way he pronounced it, referring constantly to the fact that he had been an apprentice last summer at the Brampton Playhouse.

Mike chafed under his conversation, partly because of her dislike for Taylor, partly because of the news that was almost bursting her insides. At last he got out.

As they drove off, Mike gave vent to her feelings. "There goes a prize jerk," she said.

"Taylor's rather nice when you know him," Pat said. "And he does know all about the the-ah-tah!" Pat gave the word a flippant twist, imitating Taylor. The two sisters enjoyed their laugh at Taylor's expense.

"If he had said that word once more," Mike wound up the discussion, "I planned to cram it back down his throat." She took a deep breath. "Pat, guess what? I've got news. Big news."

"What?"

"I'm going out to dinner tomorrow night with you'll-never-imagine-who!"

"Shirl Scofield? Anne Kovacs?"

"No, no. With a boy."

"A boy!" Pat was properly astounded. "Who?"

"Jeff Parker."

"Why, Mike, I can't believe it. I haven't been able to get a date out of Jeff Parker myself." The remark was spontaneous and Pat added, "I'm sorry. I didn't mean it the way it sounded. I was so surprised."

"I know." Mike was not offended. "I was surprised too."

"How did it happen?"

"There was nothing much to it. We finished the game. Beat the pants off Brighthaven, by the way."

"Good."

"I had a shower, taking my time. Was the last one out of the locker room and there he was, waiting for me." Mike took one hand off the wheel and snapped her fingers. "Just like that. He asked me if I was Mike Patterson, and when I said yes he said he wanted to take me to dinner. Tonight. I stalled, so he said, 'Well then, how about tomorrow?' "

"But first he asked you if you were Mike Patterson."

"Of course. We've never really met. Just gawked at each other at the Greasy Spoon. Or, to be more accurate, I gawked at Jeff."

Pat was quiet, turning away from Mike, looking out at the silhouettes of houses and trees against the moonlit winter sky. Mike wondered what she was thinking.

"Mike," she said at last. Mike grunted her response. "Please don't think I'm being mean," Pat went on. "You know I wouldn't want to say anything that would hurt you. But I don't want my sister made a fool of either."

The vague uneasiness she had felt when Jeff asked her for the date rose again in Mike, but she brazened it out. "I don't know what you're talking about."

"I'm not sure myself," Pat answered, and she sounded in dead earnest. "I'm not going to talk until I am sure. If I can prove to you that this whole thing is a gag, Mike, will you promise you won't go with Jeff Parker?"

Mike fell apart. These were the very words she had resisted in her own consciousness. She had silenced this thought when it had presented itself to her. She could not silence it in her sister. She gave the only answer she could give.

"Prove it first," she said. "Then I'll decide what to do."

THREE

PAT PROVED it. She proved it as conclusively as anyone could without getting sworn witnesses or a signed affidavit.

She did it by the simple expedient of calling up Flash Feeney. Flash attended Westbrook High. He was a born newspaperman and published his own paper which he called *Feeney's Fleet Street*. It was an amusing, bright little journal, appearing twice a month and snatched up eagerly by students of all the surrounding towns because it contained news items about themselves and their friends that did not get into school or town papers.

In addition to his own venture, Flash contributed to six or seven school periodicals as "visiting correspondent." Moreover, he did space writing for the *Brampton Crier*, the *New Sharon News*, the *Brighthaven Gazette*, the *Greenport Chronicle*, and the *Westbrook Hour*. Flash was, in short, quite a boy.

He enjoyed calling at the Patterson home, not only because Pat's popularity made it a rich source of information, but because he was devoted to Pat. His short, wiry body, topped by a clean face distinguished by a slightly cynical smile and crowned with curly black hair, was constantly seen popping in and out of the basement playroom.

"If anyone knows what's going on," Pat said to Mike as they monopolized the telephone in the upstairs hall, "it's Flash. What he doesn't know, he finds out."

Mike listened while Pat talked to him. "Flash, this is confidential. Jeff Parker from Brighthaven asked my sister for a date. Yes, my sister Mike. This afternoon after the game. He was waiting for her when she came out of the locker room. Never spoke a word to each other before. Know what's going on?"

Mike, with her ear to the telephone, could hear Flash's hoarse answer. "No, but I'll ask some questions. Give me five minutes. Ten at the most."

The telephone was slammed down at the other end. Pat and Mike looked at each other, not talking. Pat's face wore the indignant expression it had assumed from the moment she had heard about the date. All through dinner, Mike had watched her sister chafe with impatience to ferret out what was behind Jeff Parker's invitation. This was not mere officiousness on Pat's part. Mike understood that Pat had a genuine interest in her welfare. From early childhood Pat had always been the more socially informed. Under normal circumstances, Mike let Pat keep guard over her, watching in tolerant amusement.

Tonight Mike was not amused. She was worried. If she had had her say about it, Pat would not have put through that call to Flash Feeney. There was an old adage Mike liked. *Let sleeping dogs lie.* She subscribed to that theory. Especially when by waking them up, they might deprive you of a date with Jeff Parker.

It was not long before the telephone rang. Pat glanced at Mike for a moment before she picked it up, and for that moment Mike thought she saw regret cloud Pat's pretty face. Then, with swift poise, she reached for the telephone.

"Hello. Any news, Flash?" Pat turned her back on Mike, cupping the telephone with her hand, so this time Mike heard only the staccato accents of Flash's quick speech.

"Thanks, Flash," Pat said. "I'll never breathe a word."

She put down the telephone. It was a second or two before she turned toward Mike. "Maybe we ought to forget the whole thing, Mike," she said. "Maybe if you just called Jeff Parker up—or let me call him for you—and said you couldn't make it. . . ." Her sentence trailed off into deep thought. She started for their bedroom. Mike followed her and, catching up before she reached the door, swung Pat around.

"Tell me what Flash said," Mike demanded.

"Look, let's forget the whole thing, Mike. I'll call Jeff up and...."

Mike cut in. "You started this. Now finish it. I want to know what Flash said."

"Come inside first," Pat answered. They walked into their room, Pat switching on the nearest lamp. The room was arranged so that each sister could enjoy her own possessions. The walls were a soft shade of rose, Pat's choice, and Pat's side of the room was distinctly feminine with a rose-colored heirloom bedspread, a skirted vanity table, fluffy pillows, perfume bottles, powder jars, lipsticks, and mementoes of dances and parties. She still kept her favorite doll, blond and beautiful like Pat herself, sitting in her baby rocker near her bed.

Mike's side of the room was, at best, functional. She too had kept her favorite doll from childhood, a raffish sailor with a bulbous nose, a wicked grin, and huge, staring eyes. His hair was almost gone, but wisps of red suggested what it might have been. His clothes were utterly disreputable. Mike had always given her possessions hard wear. "Sealegs" was his name and he claimed the center of attention on Mike's side where a school banner and a horseshoe comprised the only other ornaments. Unless books might be called ornaments and of these there were dozens, piled up on the bed, the desk, and the chairs, or lying on the floor where Mike had tossed them.

Pat went to her desk and stood, her back to Mike, lost in thought. Pat's posture suggested humiliation and it troubled Mike, because she sensed that the humiliation was felt for her.

"Pat, will you please tell me what Flash found out?"

"He didn't find out anything. That's just it. He called several boys in Brighthaven and everyone was hush-hush about it. The date seems to be very top secret."

"There, you see. Maybe all your suspicions were false. Just plain imagination."

"That's not what Flash thinks." Pat turned, defending her previous doubts about Jeff Parker. "Flash seems to

20

think that it has something to do with the V.I.P. Club. Especially since no one will talk."

"The V.I.P. Club. What's that?"

"You know, Mike. The Brighthaven club that each year elects the ten boys outstanding for their contribution to the school. Jeff was sure to be one of these *very important persons.*"

"What's that got to do with me?" Mike asked.

"Mike, the boys who are elected to V.I.P. have to do some bold and daring act before they can become members. But they're not supposed to tell what they've been assigned to do. Sometimes it slips out. Sherm Jennings had to play his cornet every day for two weeks at five o'clock in the morning. Big Walt Benson had to ride his kid brother's tricycle to school for heavens only knows how long. Things like that get around."

Mike got the idea fast. "You think Jeff Parker has been assigned to take me out on a date. For that V.I.P. Club."

"I don't think anything."

"But Flash thinks that."

"Flash mentioned V.I.P. He says it's possible to put two and two together. This is the time of year V.I.P. names its new candidates. Flash was able to find out that all their assignments must be completed by tomorrow night."

Now it was Mike's turn to walk away, with her back to her sister. She sauntered over to her desk. It looked like a battlefield in which the victory had gone to no one. The notes for two term papers were spread around between reference books and unanswered letters. With one nervous push, she swept aside the whole mess. "So I'm an assignment for V.I.P. Club," she muttered from clenched teeth. "Dating me is in a class with playing the cornet every morning at five o'clock to wake up the neighborhood or riding a kid's bike to school." She crumpled some papers angrily into the basket and wheeled on Pat who stared over in distress.

"I'm a joke," she ranted on. "Just something to laugh at. Getting a date with me is a great big hilarious joke.

Take a good look at me, Pat. I'm unique. One of a kind. The only girl within a radius of twenty miles who has ever been an assignment for the V.I.P. Club."

"Mike." Pat's voice was soft with sympathy. "Don't talk like that. Boys are crazy. They have no sense. Even the best of them. They don't think how their pranks affect other people."

"Pranks! That's a mild word. This hurts, Pat. This cuts to the quick. I feel it in here." She stabbed her middle so viciously that it really did hurt and she let out a spontaneous, "Ouch!"

The exclamation liberated her. She saw the humor of the situation and her sense of balance was restored. Throwing back her head, she laughed heartily. Pat came over, but she did not join in the laugh.

"Mike," she said, "don't upset yourself about a rotten trick."

"It's funny, Pat. Honestly, I mean it. I can see how comical it really is."

"Well, I don't think it's a bit funny." Pat was still incensed. "Doing a thing like that to my sister!"

"Pat, you're wrong. And I was wrong to take it so seriously. Look, it is comical. Something that should go down in history. The girl who couldn't get a real bona fide date until the V.I.P. Club took notice of her." She sobered. "Pat, I must be pretty awful." She went to the long mirror on the door of Pat's closet. "Maybe I should have listened to you and Mother a long time ago. For years you've both tried to get the idea across to me that I'm a sight."

"You're not a sight. You're a fine girl. Very brainy, and we're all proud of you, Mike. You," Pat stammered for the words, "you have character."

There was reproach in Mike's voice. "Who ever heard of a boy falling for character or brains?" she asked scornfully. "It's looks they want. And charm. Charm's the thing. Read a few books and you'll find out." She hit the side of her head with her fist. "Pat, in some ways I'm smart, but in some ways very dumb. I've been reading books all my life and I haven't learned the most essential thing in the world."

"What do you mean?" Pat asked.

"I mean this. I haven't learned how important it is to be attractive. Oh, I've heard about such things, but I just never took the trouble. I couldn't be bothered. Look at me. Hair looks like a lawn mower had been run over it. Clothes? Just stuff to keep me from freezing. No color, no style. Of course, my face is something I can't help. It was wished on me."

"It's not a bad face at all. As I said, it has character."

Mike stalked over to her. "Character! If you use that word once more, so help me, I'll throttle you!"

They stared at each other and then started laughing. Mike sank down on a chair. "It's funny, you see. Those V.I.P. boys had a point. I'm as bad as playing the cornet every morning at five o'clock." She jumped up again, suddenly determined. "Pat, I'm going to keep that date."

"You're not!"

"I am. I'm going out tomorrow night with Jeff Parker."

"You can't. It will get all over Brighthaven. Westbrook, too. They'll make a laughingstock out of you."

Mike's eyes slanted knowingly. "They'll make no laughingstock of me," she said. "Let it get around, but it won't be a joke. I'm going to show up the V.I.P. Club. I'm going to make everyone who thinks I'm funny eat crow."

"How?"

"That's a very good question, Pat. I know we can't work miracles overnight. I won't be a glamour girl, but at least I can be reasonably attractive." She grabbed hold of her sister. "Is it so impossible? Is it too late, do you think?"

The expression of incredulity on Pat's face disappeared. She smiled. "It's not a bit too late," she said. "It's never too late." She stood back, taking stock. "Let's see, you could wear the red dress you've never worn because you wouldn't stand still long enough for Mother to alter it. We'll give you a fitting tonight."

"Say, I forgot all about that dress. It's not bad."

Pat nodded. "Red does something for a girl, especially a girl with brownish hair like yours, Mike. You could get

haircut tomorrow afternoon and have the ends curled.
. ll lend you a pair of pumps with heels. The black patents with the bag to match."

"Pat, you're swell."

Pat was all steamed up. "Some lipstick, some perfume. Who says you won't have any glamour?" She shoved Mike down on the vanity bench, and reached for one of her many lipsticks. "This is a good shade for you," Pat said. She bent over Mike, fascinated, absorbed in working a transformation. "There, even that much is better. It does help," she announced triumphantly.

"Pat."

"Huh?" Pat was still absorbed in her work.

"Those outside things are fine, but there's more to being attractive than that. I don't know boys the way you do, but I'm sure it must take more than fine feathers and a little lipstick to catch them. There must be things to do and say when you're with them. All those little things you've seemed to master, Pat, that make a girl charming."

Pat pursed her lips in thought. "There are certain rules, I suppose, but it's hard to name them."

"When you're with boys what do you do, for instance, to hold their attention? Lots of boys are crazy about you. It's partly because you're so good-looking, sure, but it must be more than that. There are other pretty girls who aren't half so popular."

Pat put away her cosmetics. It was a while before she spoke. Then her voice was quiet and casual. "For one thing, Mike, you might try being less critical of boys. Take this afternoon, for instance. I could tell the minute Taylor Watkins got in the car that you resented him. Even if you feel things like that, you shouldn't show them."

"Rule one," Mike counted off on her fingers. "More tact."

"And don't do everything in such a hurry. Take your time. Be more serene, more deep. Boys like to guess what a girl is like and what she's thinking. If you tell everything, they soon get tired of you."

"Rule two: Slow up and be mysterious. More like a *femme fatale*."

Pat shrugged off the humor. "Do you want me to be really honest?"

"Sure I do."

"You do talk an awful lot, Mike. Too much, honestly, and mostly off the top of your head. Whatever comes into your mind, you blab out without thinking."

"Thanks," Mike said drily. "I'll take a six weeks' course in holding my tongue."

"There, you're hurt and you promised not to be."

"I'm not hurt. I'm enchanted. This is a new subject to me. It's like learning Latin. An awful grind, but whew! What you've got when you've mastered it!"

"There, you're being sarcastic. Humorously so, but even witty sarcasm isn't always appreciated. You mustn't make a joke out of everything. Not with boys. They enjoy a sense of humor but they like it to be more subtle and never cutting. Don't ever let a boy get the idea you're laughing at *him*."

"Now that will really be work," Mike said with good-natured cynicism. "To spend a whole evening with a boy and not want to burst out laughing at him even once!"

"You can *want* to laugh at him, but you mustn't do it."

"I get the distinction. Anything else?"

"You have to act as if you're fascinated by them. You've got to pretend to be absorbed in the things that interest them even when you're almost fainting from boredom."

"Maybe it would be easier to just go ahead and faint," Mike quipped as she rumpled Pat's blond hair. "Thanks. I'm grateful to you, Pat. I wouldn't be at all surprised if this little session were the making of a new Mike Patterson."

FOUR

WHEN THE door of the Patterson home opened in answer to his ring, Jeff Parker was mildly surprised to be faced by a tall, attractive girl in a red dress, tweed coat, and black accessories.

"Good evening," he said. "I'm calling for Mike." He knew the girl in front of him was not the beauteous Pat, so he supposed it was an older sister.

"I'm Mike," the girl replied.

Jeff made a quick recovery. "Hello," he said. "I see you're ready. I've got my mother's car tonight." He smiled. "No motorcycle."

He was relieved when Mike tripped easily down the front steps beside him, not insisting he meet the Patterson family. Girls' families were an anathema to him. Fathers were always too hearty, mothers were coy, and the small fry reminded him of sticky flypaper, expecting all boys who called on their sisters to come equipped with candy, chewing gum, comic books, dolls, or model airplanes.

Jeff received his second pleasant surprise of the evening when Mike entered the car and took her seat beside him without initiating a conversation. Loquacious girls overwhelmed him. He was almost beginning to think that perhaps he had talked to the wrong girl yesterday after the basketball-game. This girl not only looked different, she acted different.

Something was on his conscience and he got it off fast. "I hope you won't mind if we drive over to Brampton after dinner and the movie. My mother's giving a concert at the Woman's Club. I sort of promised we'd pick her up." He half faced Mike as he drove along the road leading to Chimney Corner. "Is it all right with you?"

"Of course," she answered. "I'd like to meet your mother. I've heard a lot about her."

Jeff sighed. Frankly he was relieved. This girl was not going to be half so difficult as he had anticipated. She seemed good-natured and that was a quality not to be underestimated. Lots of girls might have balked at the idea of interrupting a date to give his mother a lift home.

They reached Chimney Corner without mishap. The hostess said their table was ready. As they walked toward it, Jeff could not help noticing that Mike carried her height well. He liked a tall girl to stand straight and not try to shorten herself by stooping over.

Mike asked him to order for both of them. "I think it would be fun to eat the same things," she said. She seemed to bubble over, showing an interest in the rustic atmosphere of the place, the unusual dishes on the menu, and people around them, and Jeff made another mental note about Mike. "Enthusiastic and natural. She gets a big bang out of everything she does."

He ordered fruit cup, consommé, London broil, baked potatoes, peas, a tossed salad. They'd choose dessert later.

Over the fruit cup, Mike asked him to explain the difference between the Austrian and the Italian techniques in skiing. Over the London broil, he discussed, at Mike's insistence, the schools he had attended. By the time dessert arrived, a baked Alaska chosen with care by Jeff, they were discussing basketball. Or more accurately, Jeff was discussing basketball and Mike was listening with rapt attention.

Jeff glowed, feeling a warmth he had seldom experienced in the presence of a girl. He expanded. Everything upon which his eyes happened seemed fine, and those eyes did not fail to include in their appreciation the attentive girl in the red dress across from him.

The food seemed unusually good tonight. Chimney Corner, noted for its excellent cuisine, appeared to be outdoing itself for the occasion. The conversation he was having with Mike was definitely superior to the talk of most girls. He was not aware that he had done practically all the talking and Mike, the listening, but he was very much aware of the fact that Mike Patterson seemed interesting and intelligent. She didn't hog the conversation. She didn't brag. Unlike so many girls he knew, she wasn't always pulling out a mirror and looking into it. The V.I.P. Club must have been given a bum steer in thinking this was a tough assignment, he thought. This girl's not half bad. In fact, she's rather nice!

As she answered a question he had asked, he found himself studying her. She wasn't pretty, that was for sure, but she was lively and she had personality. Her eyes were rather fine, wide-set and blue, and when her face lighted with a smile, she was suddenly attractive.

It's an off-beat face, he thought, but in a way she's even more interesting looking than that very pretty sister of hers.

When it came time to select a movie and Mike insisted that Jeff do the picking, stating that she was sure she'd like anything he did, he was completely won over.

This was too much to find in one girl. Good nature, appreciation, sympathy, and finally agreeableness.

He followed her out of the dining room watching her easy, athletic stride. The outdoor type, he thought. That's good. This is the kind of girl I can understand and get along with.

They picked up his mother at eleven o'clock. She came out the stage entrance wrapped in fur, her white hair gleaming in the dark. When Jeff introduced Mike, his mother said, "Hello, Mike. What an interesting name for a girl."

"It's not my real name," Mike replied.

"No? What is your name?"

"Michel. It didn't seem to suit me."

"Then we should call you Shelley. I knew a Michel in France who was called Shelley. Would you like that?"

Jeff noticed that Mike swallowed hard, but she managed to answer, "If you want to call me that, it will be all right."

"Did you have a nice evening, Jeff?" his mother asked.

"We had a swell time. How did the concert go?"

"Quite well. We had a full house. I love to play, but I'm always glad when it's over." Her laugh trilled out and Mike nodded, joining in. Then his mother settled back in silence to enjoy the relaxation of the ride home.

When they pulled up in front of the Parker house, Jeff's mother hesitated. "I don't want to spoil the evening for you," she said to them, "but how about coming in for a late snack? Your father's still up."

They had cookies and hot drinks, sitting around the fire. Mr. Parker came out of his study and joined them. Then Jeff's kid brother, Jim, clattered down the stairs in his bathrobe and slippers, complaining that he had been waked up and demanding a hot chocolate.

When Jim was introduced to Mike, he favored her with an intent scowl. "Who ever heard of a girl called Mike?" he asked.

"You did." Jeff shoved a cookie in his mouth. "So keep still."

"Mike's name is Michel," his mother said. "We've decided to call her Shelley."

Jim scowled darkly this time. "Aw, what do you want to do that for?" he barked. "Mike's a swell name. Besides, she looks like a Mike."

"What does a Mike look like?" Jeff wanted to know.

Jim sidled up to Mike and offered her another cookie. "She's a good egg," he announced with finality. "I like you, Mike. Don't you go and let them change your name."

Mike was still chuckling over Jim's remarks when Jeff turned his mother's car down the street on which the Pattersons lived.

"I like your mother and father," she said. "And I especially like Jim. He's cute."

"He wouldn't approve of being called cute," Jeff said, laughing. "He wants to be tough. Very, very tough." He paused. "Everyone liked you too, Mike. I could tell." He hopped out of the car and ran around to help Mike out.

They walked slowly up the flagstone path between banks of snow. It was cold and clear, a fine winter night. Jeff felt wonderfully good. He had told his mother the truth. He had had a swell time. He did not know when he had enjoyed himself so much. In the discovery of this new friendship, he had almost forgotten how the evening had begun, the secret skullduggery that had brought him and Mike Patterson together.

The door of the Patterson house was unlocked and Mike stepped inside. Before she could turn around to dismiss him with a hasty "thank you" as she apparently intended to do, he followed her in. She stood there watching him, a question in her alert blue eyes.

"Did I do the wrong thing?" he asked.

"No, it's cold outside. It won't hurt to get warm."

He took the measure of her, wondering. He wanted to kiss her. Some girls expected a good-night kiss, some did not. So he stood there wondering. He had a feeling that kissing Mike Patterson would be one of the nicest things that had happened to him in this evening of surprising and extraordinary events. He reached out to take her in his arms.

She drew back. The movement surprised him, not because of its element of recoil but because of the expression on her face. She seemed upset and confused, even angry.

Then her words troubled him more than her face. "Was that part of the assignment, too?" she asked. "To get a kiss?"

"What—what assignment?" he stammered.

"The V.I.P. Club assignment."

Now it was his turn to recoil. He fell back against the door, feeling for the knob, wanting to run from the house. But he did not run, he stayed and faced her anger.

"You knew!" he exclaimed. "You knew all the time." It did not matter that he was giving away his secret assignment. All that mattered was what was said here, what happened here tonight, this moment, between Mike Patterson and him.

"Yes, I knew."

"You came along just the same." She nodded, some of the anger fading. "Why did you do it?" he asked.

"I had to. I had to prove something to myself, Jeff."

"I'm sorry." He was stammering again. "I'm—I'm awfully sorry, Mike. How can I explain a thing like this?"

"You don't have to. I came tonight because I wanted to."

He did not ask her what it was she wanted to prove to herself. He felt he had no right.

"I guess you don't want to kiss me good night, Mike," he said.

"It isn't that I don't want to, Jeff." All her anger was gone. "It's just that I wouldn't want a thing like that to be part of a gag." She whispered a quick good night and half pushed him out the door.

His mother was still up when he got back, sitting in front of the fire, her slippered feet stretched out toward the hearth.

"Hello, Jeff," she said, looking at him. "Or should I say good night?"

He didn't answer.

She went on. "That was an interesting girl, quite natural and refreshing, Jeff. How did you meet her?" Still no answer came from him. "You must bring her to dinner some night. Would you like that, Jeff?"

"Oh, for Pete's sake, Mother, lay off!"

She jumped up. "Jeff, what's the matter? What's wrong?"

"Everything's wrong. Everything's the matter!" He was bellowing, thinking that by shouting he could stifle some of the outrage that stirred within. "She's an interesting girl all right. She's a swell girl. But she'll never even speak to me again, so how can I ask her to dinner?"

"I don't understand, Jeff. I thought she liked you very much. Just the way she looked at you."

"The heck she likes me!" He faced his mother, determined to tell her. He had to tell someone or he would explode right here in his own living room.

"I dated her for a gag, Mother. For the V.I.P. Club. Evidently some jerk thought she was a prize wallflower and dreamed up this date as a joke on Mike Patterson and Westbrook High School. The joke's on me instead. Mike found out. Before she even accepted the date, she found out. And she was a good enough sport to come just the same."

His mother's face showed plainly the distress she shared with him. "Jeff," she said, "that's too bad. I'm sorry."

"Me too. But being sorry doesn't help," he thundered. "Being sorry doesn't help anything."

31

FIVE

FOR TWO days Mike talked nothing but Jeff Parker. Her sister Pat was the logical recipient for her confidences and she poured these out at length. She relived the events of that memorable evening many times, recounting everything they ate, everything she said to him. She described Mrs. Parker and Mr. Parker and young Jim. She elaborated upon the Parker home which had made a solid and lasting impression.

"The living room is as big as our whole downstairs," she told Pat. "There's a color scheme. Everything sort of blends. Instead of a lot of little rugs, there's carpeting from one wall to the other. And paintings on the walls. A grand piano at one end with a vase of fresh flowers on it. And Pat, the wonderful thing is the way everything is in place. Just like something in the movies or a play. At first I was almost afraid to sit down."

Pat was more nonchalant. "Ted Stivers has a home like that," she said, shrugging. "I've been there lots of times for parties."

"I've never been in any place like it," Mike said. Then, wistfully, "You know, I think we ought to try to do something about this place. Maybe I should begin with my part of our room. Look how plain it is. Maybe if I got a new spread for my bed and some gadgets for my dresser and some pictures for the walls. And cleaned up those piles of books...." Her voice trailed off as she speculated on other things she might do.

Pat came over and gave her an affectionate squeeze. "Take it easy, Mike. The first date always goes to your head. Especially when it's with someone like Jeff Parker. That kind of boy is dynamite."

"What kind of boy is he, Pat?"

"I don't know him very well, so perhaps it's not fair to judge."

"Go ahead. I want you to say what you're thinking."

"He seems a bit aloof. Reserved is the word, I suppose. They say he tries to be like the rest of the boys, but I don't think he carries it off. Someone said that's why they're living here in this part of Connecticut, because the schools are good and Jeff wanted to go to public school. I wouldn't say he's snobbish exactly, but I think he's careful. Careful what he says and does. Careful whom he picks for friends. I think he'd be very careful of the kind of girl he'd let himself grow fond of."

"Can you control a thing like that, Pat? Can you honestly decide whom you'll be fond of? The way you decide whether you'll have grape jelly or marmalade for breakfast?"

Pat stared at her, hard and long.

"You've really got it bad," she said. Mike turned away. "Take a word of advice from an old hand at this boy-meets-girl stuff, Mike. Go easy. You can hurt yourself. You can hurt yourself awfully bad." Mike didn't answer and Pat took both Mike's hands in hers.

"Mike, if I tell you something, you won't get angry, will you?"

"If I do I'll get over it."

"It's about Jeff and another girl."

"What girl?"

"You wouldn't know her, Mike. She lives in Brighthaven, but she doesn't go to school there. She goes to Miss Covington's School."

"Miss Covington's!" Miss Covington's was a private school in New Sharon. Mike had driven past it many times. It was a vast estate that had been turned into a fashionable private school for girls. Some of them lived in the dormitories. Others whose homes were near attended during the day. Mike had her own candid opinion of the girls who attended Miss Covington's. She had seen them, en masse, descend upon Westbrook on a Saturday morning for lunch and then a movie. She had seen them walking in tight little groups, with their good conservative clothes, their air of security, and what to Mike seemed their self-satisfied, almost arrogant manner.

She didn't like them for another reason. They wouldn't enter into the interschool sports of the county. In this, Miss Covington's was different from Maple Lawn, another private school, which was very happy to play basketball, field hockey, and even softball with the public schools.

Mike had made up her mind long ago. Miss Covington was a snob and so were her students. Every time Mike saw a group of Covington girls in jodhpurs and riding jackets and hunt caps riding their horses along the back road, she would think, Just a bunch of snoots. That's what they are. Grade-A, bona fide snoots.

It was unthinkable that Jeff Parker, the boy of Mike's choice, could have anything to do with one of these girls and she said so.

"I don't believe it, Pat. It's just a story someone has spread."

"You've got to believe it, Mike. I've seen it with my own eyes, and what I haven't seen, I've heard. From reliable sources."

"Convince me if you can," Mike answered scornfully.

Challenged, Pat let loose.

"To begin with, I haven't been to a single school dance at Brighthaven without seeing Jeff with her. And if that's not proof enough, every Friday night, when I'm out on a date, we usually wind up at Susie's Beanpot."

"I know the place," Mike said ironically. Everyone knew Susie's. Pat was right about one thing. If you had a Friday night date within a radius of fifteen miles, you ended up at Susie's.

"Jeff's there with her," Pat went on.

"Every Friday?"

"At least every other Friday."

"Every other Friday doesn't mean they're going steady," Mike was reluctant to give in to Pat's argument.

"If it's not going steady, it's the next thing to it."

Mike walked away from Pat, standing with her face to the wall.

"What is she like?" she asked.

"Medium brown hair, big brown eyes, a rather large mouth, but a pretty smile. Clothes that are simply out-of-this-world. I wouldn't call her beautiful, or even cute, but she has a certain charm. The boys keep looking over at her."

"You've told me what she looks like. What is she like herself? As a person, I mean." Mike was forcing the words from a lumped-up throat. "Or maybe you don't know."

"Yes, I know. I've asked questions. She's that kind of girl. When you see her, you want to know more about her."

Mike almost choked on the question because she knew what some of the answer must be. "What did you find out?"

"She hasn't had a happy life. Her mother married a second time after she was left a widow. She married for money, they say. The new stepfather is a hard man to get along with. He's short-tempered. They say he and his new stepdaughter don't get along very well."

"But what is she like—the girl herself, the girl Jeff Parker dates?"

"She's a chaser."

"A chaser?"

"A girl who runs after boys. A couple of years ago it was a boy in Westbrook. Now it's Jeff. They say she won't let him alone."

"What's her name?"

"Charleen Morgan."

"A pretty highfalutin name," Mike grunted.

"She's a pretty superior girl."

Mike grunted again. She was thinking. Charleen Morgan. She could visualize this girl she had never met. A girl who had charm, not beautiful, but a smart dresser and with the attractiveness that could turn the heads of boys toward her. A girl with money. A girl who went to Miss Covington's. A girl who rode horseback, maybe even

35

owned her own horse, and who lived in a bigger and better house than even the Parkers. Mike saw her. She was a live creature, moving around in Mike's consciousness, playing a hard game of tennis with Jeff, swimming at the country club with Jeff, skiing with Jeff, dancing with Jeff, flirting with Jeff. Mike could hear her voice, the low, husky voice of a siren speaking in the cultured tones that were taught at Miss Covington's school.

A chaser. A girl with enough self-assurance to go after the man she wanted.

Pat put her hands on Mike's shoulders and swung her around. "If I were you, Mike, I'd try to forget Jeff Parker. I honestly think you made a mistake to go out on that date. I don't think you'll ever hear from him again. You're my sister and I love you. I don't want to see you hurt. Forget him, Mike. He's not your kind of boy and you're not his kind of girl."

Mike was seldom one to follow the advice of anyone, even her own sister, but she had to admit that Pat's remarks about Jeff Parker merited some consideration. She tried, she honestly tried to forget Jeff and that one momentous evening.

She found it was not so hard as she had expected it would be. One evening, however eventful, was hardly enough to pin one's dreams to. Especially when that evening had been instigated as a gag.

There were pressing events at school like midterm exams and theme papers that engrossed her attention. There was something even more compelling than scholastic events. There was the urgency of a basketball season that had suddenly become highly explosive.

That was the trouble with basketball. You could never tell from the way the season began just how it was going to shape up. This one, for instance, had begun fine. Everything had indicated that so far as Westbrook was concerned the winning of the county tournament would be a pushover.

Greenport, usually their biggest and toughest opponent, was suffering from the common malady of a new, untried coach. The new physical education teacher was young and attractive and inexperienced. She did everything wrong. Her team showed the effects of inadequate coaching.

Brampton, also big but not so tough, was always a threat, but this year seemed to be an off year for them. Nobody was sure what the trouble was although everyone was glib with guesses. It couldn't be Brampton's coach. She was an old-timer, a veteran athletic coach, and the girls were crazy about her. Her name was Miss Disbrow and the girls affectionately dubbed her "Dizzy." Dizzy was patient and understanding, possessor of a sprightly sense of humor, thoroughly seasoned in her job. It wasn't the girls either. Their team remained much the same as it was last year with the varsity having carried along an almost unchanged line-up. Yet something was wrong with Brampton when Westbrook first played them. Westbrook trounced them soundly with a score of twenty to five.

New Sharon was small and scrappy, with usually one or two outstanding players who rallied the team on to victory. This year, illness and injury to valued players had made inroads early in the season. Their best forward was out with a bad arm. Just one tough break like that could throw a team for a loop and New Sharon had taken that break in the worst possible way. They came out on the basketball court, oozing self-pity from every pore. The result was pathetic basketball. You couldn't drop them in the basket with one hand while you wiped tears from your eyes with the other. Their whole game was as droopy and drippy as their mental atmosphere. Westbrook gave them a shellacking, thirty-eight to three.

Brighthaven, of course, was in really bad shape. They had practically a whole new team, as Mike discovered during that first game, with not a natural player in the lot.

That's the way the season had begun, and a rollicking season it promised to be for Mike and her teammates. They were practically hugging that silver tournament cup to their sweatshirts already. All they needed was time. The breaks were all with them.

Mike was more cautious than her teammates in her

acceptance of a tournament cup they had not yet earned. This caution earned her the name of pessimist. Pessimist she was if watching warily for some turn of fortune for the other teams was to be classified thus. Pessimist she was if insisting, as acting captain, that they keep up their practice and strengthen their game to the hilt was an indication of cynicism.

She knew a thing or two about what was so lightly referred to as "luck." It just wasn't. There were things called "breaks" perhaps, but the thing that annoyed her about them was the whimsical way they all came or didn't come at once. Luck was a frivolous and flighty creature at best, even if you believed in her which Mike did not. Overwhelming good luck today could be whisked by a flip of the wrist into overwhelming bad luck tomorrow, if you subscribed to such theories. Mike considered it the better part of wisdom to disdain luck, good or bad, and be ready for any contingency. As acting captain of her team, Mike was in a position to give orders.

Her teammates pooh-poohed her, mocking her earnestness. "Practice!" they would bellow in imitation, assuming Mike's stance and stride. "That's what we need. Practice!"

However, when Mike stormed through the locker room, shouting "Come on, lazybones, get out there and toss that ball around. Miss Yates is waiting," they got a move on. They did more than move. They ran. Big Mike Patterson was a little like a roaring lion. A lion might never become a really popular animal, but its roar was not to be ignored. Besides, she was the highest scorer on the team, and the Westbrook girls had that peculiarly American drive to win.

Mike's determination not to let her team get swellheaded over their victories proved to be a prophetic move.

Their first bad break came when they played Brampton the second time. Brampton had always been a good team. There was nothing actually wrong with their coaching, their players, or their game. They merely needed to find it out, and the day they played Westbrook at Brampton they did find it out, shaking off the jinx that had hovered over them.

Mike felt something brewing in the air on the bus ride over to Brampton, a certain tenseness and restlessness which she did not like. The Westbrook girls were too noisy, too full of high spirits. Whooping it up was all right when the game was over and the victory won. Mike liked the trip over to be reasonably relaxed. It was better to save your energy for dropping them into the basket.

The Brampton girls were already in the large gym warming up. Mike ran down to the dressing rooms with the rest of her team, followed by the screams and shouts of the Brampton players as they practiced passing and tossing the ball in. While she put on her suit and sneakers, the premonition stayed with her, nagging her, because she could not understand what it was all about.

The moment she ran out on the floor, she felt something was wrong. She glanced over the court, noting the long line of Brampton girls in their orange and black uniforms. They were laughing and joking, showing off a bit as they came up to catch the ball and have their shot at the basket.

Then Mike saw what had happened. The stands on the Brampton side were full. It looked as if more than half of the school enrollment had turned out for the game. A cute cheerleader in an orange and black fan skirt ran out on the floor. A dozen other cheerleaders joined her. The familiar whirr, like that of a bullet whistling through the air, the sound which preceded all Brampton cheers, rolled out into the gym. It was their famous cry for victory.

So that was it! Brampton was staging this demonstration of moral support to bolster the courage of the team. It rattled Mike. The situation was unprecedented. Few students ever turned out for girls' basketball games. The boys' night games were the ones that drew the crowds. Most of the time the girls played to almost empty gyms.

Other Westbrook girls were whispering about it, tossing remarks to Mike from the side of their mouths. Everyone was upset.

Mrs. Andrews was the referee. She blew the whistle and tossed the ball to Shirl Scofield who caught it for Westbrook in the center circle. Shirl pivoted, looked, then used an overhead pass, hurling the ball toward Deedie Camp, another Westbrook forward. But before Deedie could jump for it, a lanky Brampton guard got the ball and hurtled it back into Brampton territory.

Brampton used zig-zag passing and got it fast to a six-footer near the basket. She reached up and tapped the ball in as easily as if she were dropping a scoop of ice cream into a glass.

A roar went up from the Brampton side of the stands. The whistling bullet that began their cheer jarred Mike. She glanced at the scoreboard. Brampton 2, Visitors 0.

Again Shirl Scofield went in to the center circle for the ball. Again she pivoted, looked, and overhead passed it to Deedie Camp. Again the lanky guard outjumped Deedie and sent the ball back to Brampton. The skinny giant under the basket reached for it and scooped it in for another two points. Brampton went wild. The noise split Mike's ears.

Mike backed up to Shirl. "They've got a basket-hanger," she said. "That six-foot bean pole won't budge from the spot. That's their whole game. The only way to lick it is to keep the ball over here."

"But how?" Shirl wailed.

Mike took a quick look at her guard, legs spread apart in a defiant pose. She wasn't any taller than Mike and she looked a lot more sluggish.

"Forget Deedie for a while. Her guard is too good. Better feed them to me."

Shirl ran into the center circle and caught the toss. She turned, hesitating. The ball zoomed toward Mike. Mike jumped for it and got it. She pivoted, dribbled, feinted a pass to Deedie, confusing her own guard on the play. Mike pulled her right arm back, holding the ball with the grace of a javelin thrower. She paused, judging her time and distance. Then she hooked it, from way out in center court. The ball teetered on the rim and dropped in. Mike could hear the exclamations of surprise from the Brampton players. Their gasps were lost in the furor of protests

40

from the Brampton rooters. They screamed and yelled, but there was no whistling bullet ricocheting against the walls of the gym.

Mike tightened the belt on her suit and strode over to the end line. Shirl glanced over and they exchanged nods. If Brampton could basket-hang, Westbrook could hook them from center court. You paid your money and you took your choice. Shirl grinned and Mike clenched her hands over her head in a symbolic handshake.

The game went like that. When Brampton caught the ball in the center circle, they tossed it to their basket-hanging bean pole. When Westbrook caught it, it went to Mike. She hooked them in. The score at the end of the third quarter was twenty-four to twenty-four. It looked as if nobody was going to win.

At the beginning of the fourth quarter Shirl Scofield, winded by a hard whack from a poorly directed ball, was taken out. Miss Yates, looking over the Westbrook team on the bench, decided to send Lynn Craig in.

Mike groaned. Lynn was fine, she would be a great player by the time the season was over, but it was bad judgment to use her now. Mike could see back of Miss Yates's decision to use Lynn. She was quick, nimble on her feet; she had a good eye for baskets. But she was still too green to be thrust into a nip-and-tuck game at a critical moment like this. A battle-scarred veteran like Pixie Dunn would have been a better choice. Pixie was erratic on baskets. She didn't have the zing Lynn had, but she was as immovable as the rock of Gibraltar. Even an earthquake couldn't unnerve her.

Lynn came in, letting her eyes rove nervously over the court. She was as sensitive as a race horse and built a little like one too, lean and hard and brown.

Mike felt sorry for Lynn. She was the kind of girl you could easily feel sorry for. Her fair hair had a decided reddish cast and it curled tightly over her head. Her chin was firm and said its owner could take a lot of punishment without squawking. Her eyes were green, bright and eager. She was hard and tough-looking outside, but you knew she buckled up quickly under criticism. She was the kind of kid Mike always wanted to protect.

41

Mike wanted to protect her now, to take her out of this game before it was too late. She was going to learn plenty and she was going to learn the hard way.

Mike's antennae were feeling the atmosphere around her. This was just the break Brampton had been waiting for. She had played too many basketball games not to know.

Mike sidled across the court as if she were expecting the ball to come this way. Actually, she wanted a word with Lynn.

"Take it easy, Lynn," she said. "Don't get rattled. Don't pay any attention to anything anyone says to you. You've got just one thing to remember. When you get the ball, feed it to me. They're basket-hanging over there and that's the only way to buck them."

Lynn nodded, but she bit her lip. Mike doubted that what she had said had reached home. The kid was too jittery. Even if she had heard, she'd forget. That's the way the roar of the crowd and the tension of the game worked on a greenhorn.

Brampton scored another goal, making the score twenty-six to twenty-four.

Lynn took the center circle. Mike watched her. She had a stricken look. In an ordinary game, without the grandstand hullabaloo, she might have stood a chance. Today the Brampton gym was bedlam, a fury of sound. The Brampton rooters chose this moment to let go one of their jungle yells and Mike saw Lynn shake. There were hisses and catcalls for Westbrook.

On their side, the smattering of Westbrook fans tried to raise a feeble cheer, but it was lost in the boos from the other side.

This was not bad sportsmanship. It was just tactics. If the tables had been turned, Westbrook might have tried the same thing. Brampton had brought out its rooters in full force with a job to do. They were there to pump lifeblood into their own team and intimidate the visitors. It was part of the game. Nobody paid any attention. Nobody but rookies, and Lynn was not only a raw recruit, but a sensitive one at that.

Her chin was thrust out. She would take it even if it killed her, but her eyes were moist. Mike wanted to rush over and throw her arms around Lynn and tell her not to mind. She wanted to scream at the roaring crowd, "Shut up, you dopes. Let the kid alone. Can't you see she's not ready to take it?"

She didn't rush out. She didn't scream. She stood there, her hands clenched at her sides, anger soaring up inside her, anger for Lynn. She waited for the ball. When it came, she'd show them. She'd hurl it so hard that it would pull down the backboard.

Only it didn't come to her. She stood there waiting while Lynn tried to make up her mind. She stared blankly from Mike to Shirl, undecided.

"Here!" Mike yelled, clapping her hands. "This way, Lynn." But her cry was lost in the noise in the gym and even if it had reached Lynn, she would not have heard. Her eyes were panicky with indecision. She let the ball go, a blind, crazy pass.

It was anybody's ball. Brampton got it and sent it back to their basket-hanger. The string bean whose arm worked like an ice-cream scoop dumped it in.

Twenty-eight to twenty-four in favor of Brampton.

The Brampton rooters boomed their appreciation, politely thanking Westbrook for the goal.

Lynn buckled up, recoiling as if she had been struck. She didn't understand that this was merely her initiation to interschool sports. She knew only that she was trapped, caught up in her own inexperience. From then on she did everything wrong. She was like a hunted animal, fleeing from something she couldn't understand, from something she couldn't even see. And with her own fear, she trapped her teammates.

The game ended thirty-seven to twenty-four in favor of Brampton.

Lynn did not join the circle of Westbrook girls when the buzzer announced the end of the game. Mike saw her run for the staircase that led to the dressing rooms. Breaking from the circle herself, Mike ran after Lynn. On the stairs, someone grabbed her arm. It was her sister Pat.

43

Startled, Mike exclaimed, "I thought you were rehearsing for the school play."

"Miss Bowman called the rehearsal off early. I came over for the last quarter of the game. It was awful."

"You saw what happened to Lynn?"

Pat nodded. "Why didn't Miss Yates take her out?"

"Miss Yates is a swell coach," Mike said slowly. "She's got one big fault. She believes everyone should learn the hard way." She broke away from Pat. "I've got to get hold of Lynn and talk to her."

"Got the car?" Pat nodded. "Good. Wait around. Maybe you can take Lynn and me home."

Mike found Lynn in a corner of the dressing room, huddled against the wall crying. Fortunately the place was empty. The girls from both teams were upstairs in the cafeteria having hot chocolate and cookies, a gesture toward interschool sportsmanship.

"Lynn," Mike said.

The curly reddish blond head was bowed. All Mike could see was the tip of an upturned nose. The sobbing was awful to hear and it tore the heart out of Mike.

"Lynn, look up; I'm your friend." She reached over and took the kid's chin, forcing her face up. "No matter what happens, never hang your head. There's nothing to be ashamed of."

"I—I—pl-played a rotten game."

"That's right, you did." The sobbing increased in volume. Lynn's shoulders heaved, her chin shook in Mike's hand. "But you'll never play a rotten game again." The sobbing eased up as Lynn contemplated the remark.

"I—I—d-don't kn-know what y-you mean."

"I mean you learned a big lesson. Fast. You'll never have to learn it again. You learned the price you pay when you let yourself get gripped by fear."

"I'll be afraid ev-every t-time I—I play."

"You will not be afraid. You're too smart. Of course I can't speak for our coach you understand, but Miss Yates is a pretty clever teacher and I think she wanted you to learn a lesson. She likes to win as much as the rest of us, but she wants us to learn a few things besides how to play good basketball."

"Wh-why d-did she l-let me play when I was so awful?" The last word ended in a wail.

"You weren't awful. You were just new. You'd never played in front of a crowd. You got stage fright. I think Miss Yates knew what she was doing. That's why she didn't take you out. She felt it was more important for you to learn to stay in that game."

"But I—I lost the game for Westbrook. It was all my fault."

"That's egotism," Mike said scornfully. "We would have lost anyway. You aren't that important."

Lynn gulped, swallowing hard. She stared at Mike. "You make me feel better," she said. "You really are my friend aren't you, Mike?"

"Look, let's get out of here," Mike said. "The gang will be crowding in soon. Let's find some place where we can talk." Lynn started to gather up her things. "Never mind those. We'll come back later for them. My sister's got our car. We'll drive you home."

Like a docile puppy, Lynn followed Mike out of the locker room. The women's athletic office was not safe. Coaches would be milling in and out. Mike paused outside a door, half open, labeled "Emergency Room."

Mike took Lynn inside and sat her down. She gave her a handkerchief and got some soap and water and washed her face. She made her comb her hair and put some powder on her nose.

"Feel better?" she asked.

Lynn nodded. "Mike."

"Yes?"

"Do you think Miss Yates will ever let me play again?"

"Sure she will. You're a good player."

"Why do you like me, Mike?"

"Because you're a real greenhorn."

"That's no reason for liking anyone," Lynn said.

"And because you remind me a little of myself."

"You never played a bad game of basketball in your life, Mike. Everyone says you're tops."

"Maybe so. But I do know what it means to be scared," Mike said. "I used to be real scared of lots of things."

"Like what, for instance?"

"Like the way people talked to me. Like the things they said to me. Like the way they looked at me. And whether they liked me. And if they didn't, why didn't they? And myself. Now that's the primary thing I was scared of. Myself. I wasn't anybody. I was a great big nothing in a world full of important people. Me, I was nothing. That used to frighten me. A thing like that can get you pretty scared when you think about it a lot."

"I—suppose—it—can," Lynn said thoughtfully. "What's the rest of the story?"

"It ends very abruptly," Mike said. "I decided not to be afraid any more."

"Can you decide not to be afraid?"

"I did. I gave myself a talking to. 'Look here,' I said, 'now these people you're petrified of are just human beings. No better, no worse than you. They don't mean one single bit more in the big scheme of things than you do. Don't be afraid of their faces and their voices. Don't care so much what they think about you. Just be yourself.' "

"Is that all? It was as easy as that?"

"Anything is easy when you settle it first inside yourself. That's where everything begins. Both the good and the bad. If you fail, you fail inside first. If you succeed, you start inside yourself. Take you, for instance. You're thinking of yourself as a greenhorn. You haven't any experience you're telling yourself. You're nervous. You get rattled easily. You try too hard and then you go to pieces. All the time you're talking to yourself. Things like that. Bad things that aren't helping you. All the trouble starts inside you."

"You know, Mike, there's a lot of sense to what you say."

"Sure there's sense to it, you poor fish," she said. "I had to learn too. The hard way." She stared at Lynn and saw her mouth turn up at the corners in a tentative smile. Mike grinned and she grinned back.

"You're nice, Mike," she said. "You're a very swell girl."

SIX

JEFF PARKER telephoned Mike that evening. She was sitting in the living room, her legs stretched out in front of her, watching a television program. When the telephone rang, she paid no attention. It was probably for Pat.

But Pat did not stir from the couch where she was managing to write a history paper, watch television, do a crossword puzzle, and pin her hair in curls at the same time. Their father answered the insistent ring.

"Yes?" he bellowed. "Who? Mike. Oh, Mike!" His voice thundered along the hallway and into the living room. "Mike! He says his name is Jeff Parker."

Mike's hands were trembling as she picked up the phone.

"Hello."

"Hello, Mike. Are you still mad at me?" Jeff asked.

"I wasn't ever mad at you."

"I called to apologize once again for what happened. I mean, well, for the gag. I'm awfully sorry. I honestly am, Mike."

"You don't have to apologize for anything."

"You're a very good sport."

"Thanks."

"I didn't call only to apologize. I called about something else." A pause. She would have helped him out if she had known how, but her social experience was not equal to this sudden switch of tactics. He went on. "I want a date, Mike. A real date with no strings attached."

"You mean just to make things right. As if it were part of the apology."

"No, I don't mean that at all. I want to see you again.

47

I've been thinking about you. You sort of stayed with me. Will you go out with me?"

"Where?"

"Anywhere you like."

She thought it over. "I don't know where to say."

"Then I'll say for you. We could go skiing this Saturday, if you're free in the afternoon. Have you got skis?"

"A secondhand pair my brother Ronnie got for me. They're nothing much to look at, but I can slide downhill on them."

"Good. We could ski for a couple of hours. Then afterward I'd like you to do a special favor for me." She waited for Jeff to say what.

"My mother wants you to come for dinner Saturday night." Mike felt for the telephone chair and sat down. Jeff was still talking. "You made quite a hit with my family, especially my kid brother. He keeps saying, 'For the love of Mike, why don't you ask Mike over here again?'" He laughed. There was a pause and then Jeff said, "Don't you want to come over for dinner, Mike? If you don't, we could. . . ."

She cut in. "I'd like it. Very much."

She heard the sigh of relief on the other end. "You're a swell sport, Mike. This won't be our last date. See you at three Saturday. Dress warm. Double sweaters under your jacket. It gets cold up on Rolling Giant."

Mike put down the telephone. She was too stunned to move. It couldn't be happening to her. Yet it was. Here she was and there was the telephone and Jeff's voice was still ringing in her ears.

Then suddenly she threw off the shock. She jumped up. A great roaring laugh began inside her and rolled to the surface. She ran to the living room as she laughed. She stood there, framed in the doorway, looking around at Pat and Mom and Dad.

"What ails you, Mike?" her mother asked.

Pat came over and shook her. "Whatever Jeff Parker said to her, it made her hysterical."

"Hysterical, my eye," Mike roared. "Jeff Parker's taking me skiing Saturday. And after that he wants me to have dinner at his house." She acted out the invitation, mimicking Jeff. "Would I as a *special favor* have dinner with his family?" She grabbed hold of Pat, dancing around the living room with her.

"Will I?" she shouted at the top of her voice. "You bet your eye-teeth I will!" Then, with sly humor she sobered. "It'll be an awful bitter dose of medicine to take, but I'll sure try to get it down."

At five minutes to three on Saturday, Mrs. Parker's car turned into the Patterson driveway and bounced to a stop. Mike was standing on the breezeway, waiting. Before Jeff could disentangle himself from the front seat, the rear door was thrown open and a half pint of a kid in a dark red ski suit and a white cap hurled himself out.

"Hi," Jim yowled, running toward her. "For the love of Mike it's swell to see you again."

"The pleasure is all mine," Mike grinned, waving to Jeff who approached with more caution.

"You got your skis?" Jim screamed everything, apparently feeling that this was the only way he could impress his hearers with the importance of what he was saying. "You got your mittens and your poles and everything?"

Mike nodded toward the stuff on the breezeway. "Everything," she said, good-naturedly. "What about you, Jim?"

"Sure. Sure thing. I got everything too," Jim screeched. "Let's go."

Jeff's ski suit was a more sober gray but his cap and mittens were yellow. He picked up Mike's skis, nodding toward his brother.

"I couldn't shake him," he said. "When he heard you were coming, he broke all previous engagements to join our party." Jeff smiled. "You've got yourself a friend for life. I hope you don't mind if he tags along."

"No," she said. "I like Jim. He's a good egg."

"There!" Jim said triumphantly, pouncing on her ski poles. "You see, I told you Mike wouldn't mind."

They parked the car at the foot of Rolling Giant. Jeff got out their skis and poles.

"I see you've got a stout pair of boots," he said to Mike.

"And your skis are in pretty good shape. Are you game to try the new trail?"

"The new trail?" Mike's voice sounded faint in her own ears. The afternoon's work had her worried. Jeff was a real skier, she was the rankest kind of amateur. She had been on skis just five times this year. Jeff had skied on all the dangerous slopes of Europe and Western America and Canada. He had been taught by experts. Mike had skied on the beginner's slope of Rolling Giant and she had been taught by her brother Ronnie who was a little better than she was. Mike had seen Jeff at Christmas time in the community ski meet. In the slalom he had brought cheers from the crowd. His jumps had been daring and breathtaking.

Mike could take off and ski downhill, but she spent as much time filling in sitzmarks as she did learned to do a Christie.

So, with some misgivings, she repeated her question, "The new trail, Jeff?"

"Yes, the new trail they've just blazed. It's a beauty. My father was on the committee that mapped it out. They thought we ought to have something better than just downhill skiing."

Just downhill skiing! Mike thought. If I can get down a hill on these cantankerous wooden wings without breaking my neck I'll be satisfied.

However, she did not argue with Jeff. The night she had gone out with him she had done fairly well by keeping her mouth shut and her eyes open. She might not do so badly if she tried that technique again. What could she lose? The worst that could happen to her was a few bruises.

In this philosophical decision she made one of the most fateful miscalculations of her life.

They walked—Jim and Jeff and Mike—over to the new chair tow which ran on Saturdays and Sundays to accommodate those skiers who brazened the more adventuresome heights. At the top Jeff helped Mike fasten her skis. He examined her poles to be sure they were in good condition.

"It's a long way down," he said, smiling.

Mike looked below her to the white spread of rolling hills. She shut her eyes and shuddered inwardly. She opened them again and saw specks in the valley below. Those specks were the parked cars and forms of other skiers.

"It's awfully far up," she ventured.

"We don't go straight down," Jeff assured her with zest in his voice. "We take the trail. Sort of like touring. It's about three or four miles through the hills, but of course we won't do it all today. We'll stop at the first rest station. They've got a man there on weekends, and he'll give us hot drinks and sandwiches."

"He will?" Mike said, feeling her knees buckling under her. "How considerate."

Jim was practicing stem turns and Christies a short distance off and Jeff called to him.

"Come on, monster, we're all set."

Mike watched Jim as he skied over. He skied as if he had been born with a pair of those things on his feet.

"I want to break the trail," he bawled with a cheerfulness that grated on Mike's already jumpy nerves. These Parkers and their enthusiasm for this hazardous sport were beginning to get under her skin, but she smiled bravely.

"Break the trail nothing," Jeff bellowed back. "That's a man's job. I'll go first, and you can be rear guard. We'll keep Mike between us."

That's what you think, Mike thought. What she said as she swung her poles behind her was, "Keep a lookout for the debris, Jim. Someone will have to pick up the pieces."

Jeff thought she was joking, of course, and Jim considered her sally enormously funny. He yipped like a pleased puppy.

Mike looked from one to the other. They were as innocent as possible of what was going on in Mike's mind. It had never occurred to these two veteran skiers that there was anybody who couldn't ski at least passing well. They knew that everyone was not an expert, but they accepted the ability to ski as matter-of-factly as most people accept walking.

Far be it from me to disillusion them, Mike thought.

Jeff dug his poles in the snow and crouched for the take-off. She watched him closely. Bent over, his arms back, he looked like a giant dark bird. "See you at the first hut," he called to them. "It's only a mile." He shoved off, skimming over the hard-packed snow with what to Mike was frightening ease.

"Your turn," Jim called.

She hesitated. It was not too late to tell them. She could still say, "See here, I can ski a little. I'm not exactly a total loss at this, but I'm certainly not good enough for this little jaunt. Look, Jim, I'm backing out. You go ahead and meet that great big competent brother of yours at the ski hut and give him my regards. Tell him I changed my mind and that discretion is the better part of valor."

She turned, half tempted to tell Jim the truth, but when she saw Jim's face, full of eagerness she just didn't have the heart to disappoint him. He waved confidently and she gave a weak wave in return.

"See you at the hut, for the love of Mike!"

That did it. She had to go. Jim left her no alternative. She pushed off with her poles, crouching as she had been taught to do, swinging first right, then left, as if she had been doing it all her life.

The truth of the matter was that she was petrified. Fear pushed its way in on the wings of the wind that whistled past her ears. She felt tense and stricken, in all this vastness, this rolling expanse of blinding white snow.

She could not let herself go.

An evergreen shot up in front of her and she let out a scream. In the nick of time she snowplowed and somehow or other managed not to lose her balance. She skied on, her scream stifled in her throat, her eyes straining for other evergreens.

There were plenty. When Jeff had used the word "trail," she had visions of a clear path of hard-packed snow waiting for them. No such thing. This was, or so it

52

seemed to Mike, almost primeval forest. Pines and firs came tearing at her, seeming, in her plight, to have motion and speed of their own. She just could not believe that they were stationary. They were rushing toward her, bent on devastation. She developed a clumsy method of slowing up and turning from their path. She doubted that what she was doing had any technical name in a skier's vocabulary. It was a combination of the snowplow, the stem-turn with a flip of a Christie thrown in for good measure, then a zing and a whir and a dash as she moved on.

Somewhere along the trail, her fear began to subside and was gradually replaced by perspective. She was getting into her stride. She saw the humor of what she was doing. She began to laugh softly at herself. Then, as she managed to avoid side-swiping a giant cedar she let out a roar of laughter.

"Mike Patterson's turn," she shouted to the space and silent snow around her. "Just plain old Mike Patterson's own little invention."

More quickly than she realized, she was heading toward the clearing that encircled the hut. She saw the log cabin and Jeff standing beside it and nothing, nothing in her whole life, had ever looked so welcome!

In her haste to be there, she overexpanded herself. She rushed into the clearing and tried to make a graceful Christie and slide to a stop. Her skill was not sufficient and she tumbled forward into a bank of snow, her skis sticking straight up in the air, back of her.

Unhurt, she tried to get up and couldn't. Jeff was beside her, then Jim. They pulled and tugged. She rolled over sitting in the snow, laughing hard.

"Are you all right?" Jeff asked. "You're not hurt?" He was testing her arms. She waved him off.

"I'm fine," she said. "I'm just fine." They got her up at last, and helped her off with her skis. Then she faced them both.

"See here," she said. "This has gone far enough. I'm a fraud. There's no sense in kidding you. I'm not even what you might call an amateur. I'm just a rank, unvarnished greenhorn."

"A what?" Jim asked.

"A greenhorn." Jeff pushed him aside impatiently. "Mike means she doesn't know how to ski."

Jim returned with alacrity to the scene of scrimmage. "Practically everyone knows how to ski," he said. "Even kids."

Mike reached over and patted him on the shoulder. "In the world you live in, Jim, you're right. Everyone knows how to ski, but not me. See that trail?" She pointed toward the expanse of snow over which they had just come. "I skied that by the skin of my teeth. And my nerve. Not with my skis because I didn't know enough to do that. I just ground my teeth, stifled my screams, and shot along."

"Why did you do it, Mike?" Jeff was sober.

"I didn't want to disappoint you," she said. "I knew you expected it of me." Jeff stared hard at her, not commenting.

They helped her into the hut. Jeff brought her some hot coffee. They made her sit quietly, until the bus came to pick them up and take them back to the foot of Rolling Giant.

While they were fussing over Mike, the telephone rang and the man in charge answered it. He looked over toward them. "One of you named Jeff Parker?" he asked.

Jeff walked over.

"Phone call for you." The man nodded toward the wall telephone at one end of the long rustic room.

Jeff went to the phone and said, "Hello." Then, in an annoyed tone of voice, "Oh, it's you."

Mike had a hunch who was on the other end of the line. Charleen Morgan.

"You didn't have to call me here," he said. "I told you I'd call you next week and that I'd be busy this weekend." Pause. "I can't talk here." Another pause. "Because I wanted to ski alone. That's why. I just wanted to ski alone. Jim's with me."

Whew! Mike thought. She sure doesn't mind checking up. They're not engaged. And why doesn't he tell her the truth? He must be afraid of her.

"I can't. I'm tied up tonight." Jeff was talking again. "Because. I planned to do something else. Never mind with whom." A pause and then a laugh. Whatever Charleen had said, it had succeeded in softening Jeff. "All right. I'm not mad, just busy. All right, I'll call you tomorrow. Good-by."

Jeff hung up and came back to Jim and Mike. Jim gave him a knowing look. Jeff looked troubled, but he tried to shake it off.

"If the invalid is all right now," he said, "maybe we can walk outside and meet the bus. It's about due."

Mike got up and reached for her skis. Jeff wanted to carry them but she insisted.

"I'm as strong as an ox," she said, smiling. "And just about as healthy. Don't spoil me with all this pampering." She smiled at Jeff and he smiled back, but neither of them meant the lightness they were showing. They were both disturbed by the telephone call.

SEVEN

JIM WAS so noisy on the way home that Jeff was glad when they finally reached the house. Jim was the first one out of the car. Jeff watched his brother tear into the back hallway, bawling at the top of his lungs that he was starving.

"When's dinner going to be ready?"

Jeff's mother was there to greet them. "We've been waiting for you three snowbirds. Go up and wash, Jim." Jim took the back stairs two at a time.

"Hello, Mike." Mrs. Parker shook Mike's hand warmly. "We're so glad you could come. Did you have a good time on the trail?" Mike looked at Jeff, but neither of them answered that question.

"The food smells wonderful!" Jeff exclaimed. "Boy, am I hungry!" The dining-room table, spread with a fine old lace cloth, was spilling over with good things to eat. Around a centerpiece of yellow roses were arranged casseroles of chicken and spaghetti, baked stuffed celery, creole eggplant. A glazed baked ham topped with rings of pineapple and cherries stood at one side and at the other was the brown bean pot sending out its delicious fragrance of spice and molasses. There was a large wicker tray filled with all kinds of bread—home-baked white bread, date-and-nut bread, brown bread, corn muffins. The cake and pies stood on the buffet along with the silver coffee service and the Delft blue plates and cups and saucers.

Webbsie was responsible for the fancy breads and the pastry. She was the Parkers' "help." As long as Jeff could remember no one had dared to refer to Webbsie as "maid" or even "housekeeper." She liked mystery stories, television, knitting, raising roses, and boys, but not exactly in that order. Boys, perhaps, came first, and Jim and Jeff were devoted to her. The roses on the table tonight had come from Webbsie's greenhouse, a tiny glass structure at the rear of the house which Mr. Parker had had built especially for her.

Next to his mother, Jeff preferred Webbsie to any other woman he had met. She was a good sport. She would play a game of Scrabble with him and he could invariably beat her. She shared his liking for detective stories and they kept each other informed and supplied. What one missed, the other didn't. Jeff always spent at least ten minutes of his day in the kitchen with Webbsie, sampling her pastry and discussing the possible outcome of the three or four serials they were following in magazines.

Webbsie baked the best cakes and pies in Brighthaven. Her coconut cream was so famous that people called Mrs. Parker on the telephone to beg one for every fair in the neighborhood. Personally Jeff preferred her Dutch apple pie and orange layer cake, but that was a matter of taste. Everything she cooked was delicious.

Jeff had always been curious about Webbsie's first name. She invariably signed all papers "U. Webb." When the subject was tactfully broached, Webbsie avoided the issue. Jeff gave the matter serious thought and suggested possibilities.

Ursula? Undine? Urania? Ulrica? Uda?

"My name's Webbsie," she would say, with finality. "Go get yourself a piece of that fresh-made apricot pie and be quiet."

Webbsie appeared now, bearing the relish tray, sweet pickles, watermelon rind, pepper relish, spiced crab-apples, cottage cheese. She set it down and faced Mike, clearly expecting to find out who this new girl was. Mrs. Parker did the honors.

"Webbsie, this is Mike Patterson, a new friend of Jeff's."

Webbsie grunted her acknowledgment. Then she said, "I've got a fresh-made coconut-cream pie in the refrigerator. I'll bring it out."

When she had gone, Jeff laughed. "She took a liking to you, Mike. She wouldn't have offered that coconut-cream pie otherwise. Bet you a buck that before you leave, she'll ask you if you read mysteries."

"I haven't got a buck." Mike said, grinning.

The evening turned out to be a pleasant one in many ways. They had dinner, around the fire, sitting in comfortable chairs, their trays perched on snack tables. Jeff's mother and father seemed to enjoy Mike. Tonight she was more relaxed than the first evening she had been here. Jeff's father had a dry humor which was not quickly appreciated by those who did not know him well, but Mike caught on to it from the start. Her throaty laugh rolled out into the room in response to his sallies. Mr. Parker mellowed under such whole-hearted appreciation. Jeff had not seen him in such a jovial mood in a long time.

Mike endeared herself further by asking Mrs. Parker to play for them, and by loving her music.

Jeff found himself more and more pleased at the way Mike was taking hold. It was something he could not explain, even within the secretly guarded precincts of his own consciousness. All he knew was that he wanted his family to like her. Acceptance did not enter into the picture. It was enough for him that he himself accepted her and wanted her for a friend. But it was important to have her appreciated by those close to him.

Jeff finally claimed Mike for his own, suggesting they go to the game room. Jim was immediately beside them, pleading with Mike to play a game with him. Jeff told his brother to go chase himself, but Mike interceded, saying, "Let him come along for a little while anyway, Jeff."

"For a very little while," Jeff said, glaring at Jim.

It was while they were sitting at the card table that Webbsie appeared in the doorway, beckoning to Jeff.

"Telephone," she said. "Better take it upstairs." He knew instantly who it was. Only one person would call him up on Saturday night at this time.

Before he had time to shut the door hastily behind him, Webbsie's sonorous voice boomed at him.

"It's her," she said. "*Miss* Morgan." Webbsie's pointed inflection of the "Miss" indicated how little taste she had for the lady in question. "Why can't she let you alone for just one night? It beats me how brazen girls can be nowadays. She can't hold a candle to that girl in there."

"Sssh!" Jeff said, knowing it was too late. Mike must have heard. Although the compliment was directed toward her, he wondered what she must think about this second telephone call today. It worried him. He was not ready to tell her about Charleen. There would be a right time to talk about Charleen, but not tonight, not yet.

When he returned to the game room, Mike was playing Scrabble with Jim. There was no indication that she had heard Webbsie's remark. Yet Jeff was sure she must have heard.

At last it was time for Jim to go to bed. He went protesting, almost making it necessary to grab him by the scuff of the neck and drag him out. But he did go.

So at long last Jeff had Mike to himself.

With some girls, Jeff would have felt the need to be entertaining, to suggest a game of ping-pong or honeymoon bridge, to make brilliant conversation. Tonight he did not even feel talkative, a mood so rare for him that at first it startled, then bewildered, and finally pleased him.

I feel comfortable with Mike, he thought. Even when we're quiet together. She isn't striving for anything. She's not out to get votes or make an impression. She's just herself. That's why she's so easy to be with.

They played records for a while, softly so as not to disturb the family. Jeff had the best collection of jazz records in Brighthaven and Mike was properly impressed. She had never seen or heard anything like it she assured him many times.

He played some dance music and held out his arms, expecting her to step into them. She hesitated a moment, then she joined him. She was a good dancer, although somewhat limited in her repertory of steps. He taught her the mambo and the samba. She was easy to teach, full of fun. It was a long time since he had dated a girl who dared to show enthusiasm about anything. Most of them were too busy trying to be sophisticated.

They had a late snack—although Mike swore she could not eat a thing—of ginger ale and Webbsie's pound cake in the kitchen, sitting at the knotty pine snack bar. Once again Mike bubbled over.

"I've never seen anything like this place," she said. "It's wonderful. I wish we had something like this in our house. It must be a lot of fun, living in a house like this."

"Sometimes it is," he said, "when you're with people you like. I mean when you have the friends you really want." She looked up from her glass quickly, her eyes were asking him to go on and he did go on. "It's been a terrific evening, Mike. One of the best. I feel as if it should never end." Then, for fear he had said too much, he hastened to add, "I mean you're so easy to be with. You're. . . ." He floundered, not wanting to make it too strong, yet wishing to say what was on his mind, "You're real."

It sounded wrong. It sounded stilted and artificial and all wrong. Yet Mike was pleased.

"That's the nicest thing any boy has ever said to me." She made it sound as if boys had been saying complimentary things to her all her life, yet his one halting remark had topped them all.

"Do you like me as much as I like you, Mike?"

He noticed that she flushed, and that pleased him. It meant that she was not accustomed to accept or give affection lightly.

"Oh yes," she said after a thoughtful pause. "I do, Jeff. I like you a lot."

"If you liked a boy very much, Mike, would you let him give you something, a sort of token, to show that he liked you very much too?"

She glanced away, then quickly back. "I—I guess so."

He fumbled in his pocket and pulled out a well-worn wallet that his father had bought him in Italy. From one of the pockets he took a slim silver skier and held it up.

"It's sort of a good-luck piece," he said. "Only that's not exactly the word for it. Let's just call it a token of good faith, Mike. I like you and you like me. So will you please wear this?"

She hesitated so long that he thought she was going to refuse, but she said, "I'd love to, Jeff."

He held it out. "You could wear it on a chain or ribbon," he said.

"Would you mind awfully if I wore it on my bracelet?"

"That would be swell." He went to the odds-and-ends drawer where Webbsie kept her tools and brought back a pair of pliers. The link was just big enough to permit the charm to hang gracefully from Mike's slender bangle bracelet.

"I could have it soldered by a jeweler," she said. "So it won't come off."

"That's a good idea," Jeff agreed. He touched her hand lightly. "I don't ever want it to come off either, Mike."

He drove her home through the cold winter night feeling warm and wonderful inside. He had at last found someone who understood him, no matter what he said or did, no matter how talkative or how quiet he wanted to be. He thought about Mike's bracelet, with his silver skier hanging from it. Mike did not know, she could not possibly know that this was the first time in his life he had voluntarily given anything to a girl.

It made him feel lifted out of himself, as if he were driving the car on air instead of along the concrete road between Brighthaven and Westbrook.

When they reached Mike's house he ran around to help her from the car. They walked slowly up the front walk to the door. As she turned to say good night, she smiled at him, and he knew from her smile that this time it was all right. So he took her in his arms and kissed her good night. Turning quickly, he ran back to the car. He waited until she had unlocked the door and gone inside.

Then he turned on the ignition. He whistled softly to himself. Wonderful evening. Wonderful girl. Wonderful everything.

EIGHT

IF JEFF PARKER felt as if he were driving his mother's car on air along the road from Brighthaven to Westbrook that winter evening, Mike Patterson went him one better. She walked on air. For two solid weeks while ordinary human beings went about the drab business of having breakfast, going to work or school, eating sandwiches or steaks or chops, reading newspapers, doing homework, watching television, Mike Patterson sailed serene above the confines of earth. She was *in* the world, but not *of* it.

She walked apart, a girl who had been touched by the most magical thing in human experience. She knew it was called love, but she had never dreamed it was anything like this.

It came at her like an avalanche. One moment she was walking on solid earth, a girl who liked hot dogs and double fudge sundaes, basketball and good books, western movies and serials, skirts and sweaters, long walks, bull sessions, and the color lavender. The next moment she was jarred and wrenched, pummeled and pushed, jerked and catapulted into outer space, whizzing and zooming and lurching about like a flying saucer.

She had moments of ecstatic happiness, as indescribable as they were delusive. No one, no one in the whole world —and of this she was so sure that she would have throttled anyone who contradicted it—had ever been as happy as she. She had Jeff's silver skier on her bracelet, touching her wrist, to convince her of the fact. She had his words still humming in her ears. *I don't ever want it to come off. I like you and you like me. You're real.*

It never occurred to her that these words were not an astonishing commitment of affection. To Mike they were etched in gold and purple, the most magnificent declaration of love any boy had ever made to any girl.

It is true her happiness was not unmixed. There were doubts, facts that could not be avoided. Jeff Parker moved in a world different from hers, a world of big, comfortable, beautiful homes, of families with several cars. He had traveled. He had been educated in Europe. He appeared to her to be suave and breath-taking.

Besides, there was another girl.

Whenever Mike thought about Charleen Morgan, she would glance down at the silver skier dangling from her bracelet just to reassure herself. Her intuition told her that Jeff would never have given her his favorite charm unless he was fond of her. She had heard of boys who made such gestures lightly. Her brothers joked about a boy at Yale who carried a half-dozen silver football charms in his pocket. He had never played the game, but it was part of his line to tell the girls he met that he was a football player, and every girl who struck his fleeting fancy was presented with a silver football.

Things like that could happen. It was possible that Jeff had been trifling that evening, but Mike did not believe he was.

The presence of Charleen Morgan as very real competition was somewhat harder to deny. She was a live person, no figment of Mike's imagination. Pat had discussed her with Mike at length. Charleen was seen everywhere with Jeff. She had telephoned Jeff twice on that memorable day when he had presented Mike with the silver skier. Jeff had never mentioned Charleen, and Mike could not open the subject. She had no idea how much this girl might mean to Jeff.

What made Charleen even more formidable was the fact that Mike had never laid eyes on her. It was much easier to meet competition you could see with your own eyes. Reports varied. Some said that Charleen was beautiful, some insisted that by no stretch of the imagination could she be called that. Some said she was snobbish, others that she could be friendly when she was drawn out. Some depicted her as a self-centered, frivolous play-girl who thought only of fun, of dancing, riding, skiing, swimming, and sailing; and some reported her as a victim of her stepfather's choler, a poor-little-rich-girl who needed to be understood.

How could Mike possibly know what she was really like? It was like shadow boxing, you jabbed and punched and prodded an illusive image created wholly in your own mind.

So she fretted. She permitted herself to be nagged by doubts. These were earth-weights dragging her down from the clouds in which she floated.

Jeff called her up every other day. He met her after a basketball practice and they had sandwiches at a diner and then went to a movie. He even sent her an amusing card he had found in a shop to show that he was thinking of her.

It was a romance. It was the stuff her dreams had been made of. Yet it was not enough. Something was missing. She wondered if everyone who ever fell in love had felt this way.

To her worries about Jeff were added the complications of a basketball season that had gone haywire.

Brampton had set the pace. That afternoon when Brampton had filled its side of the stands with rooters, the school had set the fashion for other high schools. If Brampton decided to support girls' basketball, the rest would support girls' basketball too.

Mike understood that this was standard high-school procedure. It was a case of monkey see, monkey do.

Therefore, to Mike's surprise, girls' basketball became big stuff. Committees were appointed to boost morale and round up the crowds. Posters calling the student body to attend games were drawn and lettered, then placed in halls and on bulletin boards. There were rallies. Prizes were offered for the home rooms that furnished the largest attendance at games. All because Brampton had started out with an off-season.

In some ways Mike found the upsurge of interest a good thing. Her favorite sport now had prestige.

Not the least of the immediate benefits derived from

the new devotion to girls' basketball was the popularity it brought to Mike. From a girl who was a lone wolf, with one major accomplishment, she became a public figure at Westbrook High. As acting captain of the team, she was drawn into every rally and committee meeting and discussion connected with the new basketball boom.

When her schoolmates discovered how good a player she was, they all but stampeded her. During the first game she played under the new policy, with the Westbrook stands filled, with the full corps of cheerleaders dancing and shouting and turning handsprings on the gym floor, with the whole school to back her up, Mike covered herself with glory. She made twelve of the Westbrook baskets that defeated New Sharon by a score of thirty-six to sixteen. The other forwards made two baskets each and the rest of the points were free throws.

The crowd cheered Mike more than any other player. Her name was on everyone's lips. She was the fair-haired girl.

"Two-four-six-eight. Who do we appreciate? M-i-k-e. Mike Patterson!"

The dazzling limelight of success was turned upon her. She tasted the sweet fruits of popularity. When the game was over, the crowd rushed to the gym floor and surrounded her, shaking her hand, patting her on the back, screaming in her ears.

"You showed them, Mike. You're our girl. You won the game for Westbrook. There's only one Mike Patterson."

Two starry-eyed freshmen shoved autograph books under her nose and asked her to write in them.

"Not just your name, Mike. Something personal. So we can show our friends and tell them we know you."

That night four boys, one of them from New Sharon, called her up and asked for a Friday night date. She told them all the same thing, that she would think it over.

She did think it over, but not in the way they might have expected her to do. She went to the room she shared with Pat and closed the door quietly behind her.

Pat was out and that was good. More than anything, she needed to be alone.

Her head was swimming and her throat, parched. Although she had hardly touched her supper, she felt butterflies in her stomach. This was in itself unprecedented. After a normal basketball game she tucked away two chops or a thick slice of roast beef, two helpings of vegetables, pie à la mode, and a pint of milk. She would do her homework, watch a little television, and then turn in for a dreamless sleep, undisturbed until her father pounded on their door to wake them up.

Tonight she felt so excited that sleep seemed as remote as a trip to Mars.

So this was popularity. This was the thing that had eluded her all these years. This was the stardust that had fallen on Pat and left Mike untouched until now.

She was not sure she liked it. Another girl might have felt only the thrill of being praised and needed, might have heard only the cries and cheers that made a somebody out of her. Yet at this very moment Mike turned from the glory and the excitement to be quiet, to think.

This could lead to something bad, she thought. Real bad. It could stir up jealousy and strife among the girls. A person could get so she thought she was a lot of things she wasn't. Just because she can toss a basketball from way out in center floor and have it bounce through a metal hoop.

Not a big thing, really. Nothing that will ever take the world by storm. Just something a lot of crazy kids want you to do so they can scream their heads off because you licked the stuffing out of the other team.

A demigod just because you've got a good eye and a strong arm and steady nerves.

Look, she said to herself. I haven't changed one bit since yesterday. Everything I am tonight, I was last night. Yet last night no one knew I existed. Those four boys wouldn't have even given me a tumble. I was the girl to assign as a gag date to a V.I.P. candidate.

I was just somebody's sister. *You know, Pat Patterson's sister Mike.*

Now I'm a somebody. Everyone knows me. Mike Patterson, the best forward on the Westbrook team. That girl who can stand out in center court and hook them in. *She's our girl.*

She slumped down on the chair in front of her desk. "I don't want dates because I can throw a basketball," she muttered to herself. "I want them because someone likes me for what I am."

She glanced down at the silver skier dancing on her wrist. It gleamed in the light of her desk lamp and she thought of Jeff. Tonight he seemed closer to her. He was something solid and secure to reach out to while she teetered on the dizzying heights of popularity.

NINE

THE DAYS that followd confirmed Mike's worst fears for her team. The premonition that had made her vaguely uncomfortable on the night of the New Sharon game was proved accurate.

Rivalry smoldered and crackled all along the line of play during practice games. In the next interschool game it burst forth into flames.

Mike knew what the trouble was. Girls weren't geared to this high-pressure athletic competition. The normal girl, no matter how good an athlete she was, just couldn't play a man's game. Put the heat on the average boy, and he fought harder, but girls' emotions were too near the surface. Mike had seen things happen on the court, things that a boy might throw off with a laugh, reduce a girl to tears.

Mike watched the Westbrook basketball team change almost overnight from a group of fun-loving, easy-going athletes into a stable full of thoroughbred horses, restive, jittery, full of temperament.

A few kept their heads. Girls like Shirl Scofield and Deedie Camp, the two other varsity forwards on the Westbrook team, were not likely to be overwhelmed by finding themselves suddenly in the limelight. They were sensible girls, attractive, going steady with boys of whom they were very fond. The bulk of the trouble stemmed from the new forwards, youngsters who were being broken in this season, like Boots Overton and Mary Melillo, and from the Westbrook guards.

Boots and Mary had high potentials as basketball players. Early in the season Miss Yates had discovered that Boots had a pivot shot that made her invaluable in playing against a long, lanky guard. Mary had a less spectacular chest shot, but it was accurate and steady in performance. Both girls would be varsity mainstays next year.

Mike liked their game and she had liked their spirit, too, until the big basketball boom came along and transformed them.

One day Boots and Mary had been likable kids, shouting at each other about boys and homework and the movie they planned to see, grateful for the pat on the back which the older forwards always took the trouble to give them. The next day, as a result of the Maple Lawn game, they became self-centered little snips with their noses pointed toward the sky.

Mike wouldn't have believed it possible if she hadn't been there to see the sudden transformation with her own eyes. Maple Lawn was the private school which, unlike Miss Covington's, entered into the county tournament. The Maple Lawn game was always a popular one at Westbrook and this year a record crowd turned out. Maple Lawn girls were good-looking. The boys enjoyed watching them and the Westbrook girls turned out to see them too. They played good basketball. The game was bound to be a humdinger.

Fate played a hand in the game by absenting Shirl Scofield from school that day and further by putting the impulsive Deedie Camp out of the game at the end of the first half on three technical and two personal fouls. That left the field wide open for the greenhorn forwards on the team. Mike chafed during the intermission, wondering who Miss Yates would send in. She was glad to see that Lynn Craig was on the benches when the new line-up was given. Boots had been playing in Shirl Scofield's place and now Mary Melillo came in for Deedie Camp.

Mike breathed more freely. She was partial to Lynn, preferred her playing to any of the other greenhorn forwards, but she did not like to see her playing during the whole second half of a tight game yet, not so soon after the Brampton debacle.

If Mike had only known! She was soon to learn that even Lynn, with her sensitiveness, might have been a better choice than Mary Melillo. Mary came into the game with a swagger that almost jogged Mike right off the court. She was like an actress who had been standing in the wings for weeks, understudying the lead part, and now she saw her chance. The star was out and she was in!

The contagion spread to Boots and together they made a swashbuckling pair, feeding the ball to each other, keeping the ball from Mike, running up an impressive number of points between them, and defeating Maple Lawn with a score of thirty-three to twelve. Mike had made ten of the points but eight of these were made during the first half. One basket was all she had been permitted to make during the last half by the pair from the substitute bench.

They laughed about it later on in the locker room, cackling their triumph to each other.

Mike overheard their conversation from the vantage point of a row of lockers behind which she had left her clothes.

"We sure put Her Nibs in her place, today, didn't we, Boots?" And the laugh that followed had an edge of nastiness in it. "Thinks she's the only star on the team. Making that big splurge during the New Sharon game. Who does she think she is?"

Boots mumbled something which Mike did not catch and Mary's voice, strident and resonant, came sailing back again.

"I'm glad we had the chance," she said. "I'm glad Shirl was absent and Deedie got herself put out. They've all treated us as if we were a couple of kids. Patting us on the back like a couple of puppies that fetched their slippers for them. Especially Her Nibs. She's too bossy. Knows too much. A very superior person with all her airs, with her nose stuck in a book and that Mother-knows-best attitude. Who does she think she is anyway?"

Mike found herself grinning in spite of the shocking misunderstanding of Mary's analysis. Nobody had patronized the two girls. Everyone had tried to encourage and help them along.

Who do I think I am? She repeated Mary's question in the first person. I don't consider myself "Her Nibs" at all.

I'm just like the rest of you, like you and Boots, Mary. Trying to find myself in the scheme of things. Feeling a little lonely sometimes. Wanting to be needed and loved. Wanting to belong. Wanting to do something well, even if it's only to hurl a good hook shot into the basket. The way you cut me out of the game frightens me. Not because you shut me out, although I didn't like that especially, but if this sort of thing keeps up girls' basketball isn't going to be fun any more.

But if Boots and Mary were getting a bit out of hand, this was nothing compared with what was happening to the guards on the Westbrook team. While the grandstand playing of a couple of substitute forwards could be annoying, the rebellious behavior of the regular varsity guards was much more than annoying. It was dangerous.

Forwards were the stars of the team, no doubt about it, and a girl with a good hook or pivot or chest shot could make a show for her team and a name for herself. They were the ones who piled up the points. They were the ones who drew the cheers and the applause. But in the long run, Mike knew that no girls' basketball team was any better than its guards.

Mike figured it this way. The work of the guards was like the skeleton of a house, hidden beneath layers of shingles and brick. But withdraw the framework of a house or guards from a basketball team and the whole thing would collapse.

The Westbrook guards had all the qualifications essential to this important position on the team. They were quick on their feet, speedy on recovery, clever in their strategy, and tall. Until now, their speed and trickiness had immeasurably strengthened the Westbrook forwards' game. Most important of all they had teamwork. Fast friends off the basketball court, they stuck together forming a tight little clique of their own, and, in this clique, Emma Gaudet was the recognized leader.

Mike had never been able to get through to Emma. In Mike's language, they just didn't "reach each other."

Emma was a leggy girl of French Canadian parentage. Her hair was black, her eyes bright blue, large, and bold.

She was pretty, with the speed and grace of a panther, and she liked to clown.

Until the turn of events that catapulted girls' basketball into the limelight, Emma had kept most of her clowning off the basketball court. She was a born comedian. When she really let go, you almost split your sides laughing.

Mike recognized Emma's talents in spite of the wall Emma had thrown up between them. Once or twice Mike had tried to pull down that wall and reach a better understanding, but she had always met with a rebuff. It was as if Emma, without reaching out a hand, had given Mike a shove away.

Yet this distance between them had never mattered in a game. Mike was a good forward. Emma, a good guard. They played together and they won the game for Westbrook whenever they could.

In the New Sharon game that had made a star of Mike, Emma showed some faint signs of the trouble that was to come. Agile and adroit, she had watched a famous comedy team of basketball players and patterned her playing technique after them.

She feinted to the right and passed to the left. She dribbled and zigzagged. The spectators were delighted. They guffawed and shrieked and howled, roaring Emma's name, "Go it, Gaudet! That's the stuff! Show us some more!"

Both the New Sharon and Westbrook stands entered into the fun, goading Emma on. It took only a little encouragement to turn her from a first-rate basketball player into a side-splitting comedian.

The same thing happened in the Maple Lawn game. Emma put on a side show of her own. It was good fun, but it wasn't particularly good basketball. It slowed up the game and rattled the players of both teams. For a professional group of players to stage this kind of show was one thing, for Emma Gaudet to do it during an inter-school tournament game was another. Mike wondered how long she would get away with it. If Miss Yates didn't crack down on her, one of the other coaches would surely crack down on Miss Yates. It made a tense situation even tenser, and something was sure to give.

It did. The crack-up came during the Greenport game. Greenport was big and they were tough and they played to win. No fooling about it.

When the Greenport girls ran on the court, dressed in solid black uniforms, black shirts, pants, and sneakers, with a touch of hunter green in their ties, Mike thought they resembled nothing so much as a bunch of female Draculas. They had toned up their game since the beginning of the season. The new coach who had made so many mistakes earlier, wasn't so new any more. The girls were used to her and she was used to her job. Much of the old Greenport self-assurance had returned.

The first quarter was not spectacular. Both teams were feeling each other out. The stands, fuller even than usual, roared for more action. The quarter ended with a score of seven to four in favor of Westbrook. Deedie, Shirl, and Mike had made one basket apiece. The free throw had gone to Mike. Their team was in the lead, but by a very narrow margin. Greenport was warming up and almost anything could happen.

During the rest period, Mike lay on her back on the floor, her hands folded under her head. Deedie and Shirl were stretched out on either side of her and just beyond Emma Gaudet, never quiet, was quipping to the guards. Back of the team, on the Westbrook side of the stands, the cheerleaders held forth.

Mike listened to their shrill cries, to the thump of their feet as they punctuated their cheers with jumps and handsprings. She made out her sister Pat's voice above the others as Pat led the group.

From the stands one insistent voice shouted, "Hey, how about a cheer for Patterson? Mike Patterson! Give her a hand."

The stands took up the cry and then Mike heard the familiar "pep" cheer. "Who are we for, who do we want, who do we know is good. M-I-K-E. Mike Patterson!"

It was routine stuff, nothing to get excited about. The stands had to let off steam and this was the way they did it. No one paid any attention. No one but Emma Gaudet. Her voice cut across the floor reaching Mike's ears.

"I wouldn't mind having a sister who was head cheerleader," she commented. "Maybe I'd get a cheer once in a while too."

Ignore it, Mike thought. Don't get riled. Let it pass and no one will be wiser.

Inside she couldn't let it pass, however, because this was the first time anyone on the varsity had said a thing like that in public. The locker-room snippiness of a couple of greenhorns like Boots and Mary was one thing. This was something else again.

Emma however was not satisfied. She was looking for trouble. Mike's silence was hardly the reaction she had been expecting.

"Some of us have friends on the cheerleader squad," she went on in a voice intended to carry, "but it doesn't do us any good. Our name has to be Patterson if we want to get anywhere around here. Between you and me, Bess," she directed her remark toward one of the other guards, "there's been too much Patterson in this school for too long. That's the trouble."

The horn called them back into play and the whole team jumped up. Mike was the last one on her feet and as she got up slowly her eyes met Emma Gaudet's. There was venom in Emma's steel blue eyes, and it was aimed straight at Mike.

There's been too much Patterson in this school for too long.

The words cut into Mike's consciousness like a barb, stinging and hurting. She tried to forget them and go back into the game.

The second quarter was as fast as the first had been slow. Greenport came in with new zest. In the first two minutes of play they tied the score, then went on to make two extra baskets. Mike glanced over at the scoreboard. Visitors, 11; Westbrook, 7. It didn't look good.

Mike hiked up her shorts, tightening her belt. She signaled Shirl to send the ball to her out in center court. She had been watching the Greenport guards and noticed that they were trained for zone defense. Let the West-brook forwards switch their court tactics and that would mean a change of guards. The Greenport guards would stick to their zones, Mike could shake off the leech who had been hovering over her during the first quarter, and she'd have an open shot at the basket.

Mike's guess was that Greenport's new coach was a stickler for zone defense, scorning the "combination" zone and man-to-man defense that would bring the leech-like guard after Mike to stop her shots.

Mike's guess was right. She ran out into the court but the Greenport guards held to their zones. Mike drew a shorter girl this time, tough, not above using shoulder and knee and elbow tactics when the referee wasn't looking, but definitely shorter. That was what Mike had been looking for.

She now had a fairly clear chance at the basket. If nothing went wrong, she could easily pile up a few points. She did. In the next five minutes of play, she made four hook shots from center court. The quarter ended so fast that Mike was surprised to hear the buzzer. As she crossed toward the door during the intermission, she looked up at the scoreboard. Visitors 13; Westbrook, 15.

It was still too close for comfort.

She went down to the locker rooms, wanting to be alone for a couple of minutes. Today the noise and screaming in the gym grated on her. The cheers from the stands followed her and she heard her name.

"Who are we for? Who do we want? Who do we know is good? M-I-K-E. Mike Patterson!"

There's been too much Patterson in this school for too long. That's the trouble.

She put her hands over her ears to shut out the sound, but she could not shut out Emma's voice, strident and accusing.

This is it, she thought. This is what I was afraid would happen. And it has happened. Almost more quickly than I expected.

"Mike!" She turned toward the door. Deedie Camp was standing there, her eyes large with excitement.

"They're fighting. It's awful."

"Who's fighting?"

"The cheerleaders. Up there." Deedie nodded toward the gym. "Pat's in the middle of it."

Mike strode toward the door, shoving Deedie out ahead of her. She took the stairs two at a time. The gym door was open and a crowd eight or nine deep stood huddled at the Westbrook side.

Mike pushed her way through. There in the middle were the Westbrook cheerleaders. At first Mike could see only the blur of blue and white cheerleader uniforms. Then she saw what was happening. Pat stood at one side, alone. Her face was scarlet, her blond hair tousled and streaming over her forehead down to her shoulders. She faced ten or twelve of the cheerleaders. The hubbub was awful to hear. Suddenly a silence fell over the crowd and the voices of the leads in this terrifying little drama pierced the big gymnasium.

"You're not fair," one of the cheerleaders shouted at Pat. "You don't know how to be fair. All you know how to do is call the cheers for your sister."

"Leave my sister out of this. This has nothing to do with Mike."

"Oh, hasn't it?" Another cheerleader stepped into the fray. "It has everything to do with her. Since she's become a star," and the word was hissed spitefully, "no one else on the team exists. Between the two of you, the school isn't big enough to hold the Pattersons."

Someone touched Mike's sleeve; she turned, only half seeing Joan Sibley, the shortest of the Westbrook guards, through the blur of emotion that clouded her eyes.

"Emma started it," Joan whispered. "I don't like it, Mike. I want you to know I'm not in on it. She stirred up her friends on the cheerleader squad. She's a trouble-maker."

Mike pushed her way toward Pat. She had to pull her sister out of this. It wasn't getting any better and if someone didn't stop the verbal battle it might develop into something worse. But before she could reach Pat, Mr. Davis, head of physical education at Westbrook, came through

76

the crowd. He went straight to the center of the trouble.

"What's going on here?" he asked. All the girls started to talk at once. He held up his hand. "This is no place for a squabble," he said. "I'm surprised at you." His eyes swept the crowd that had gathered. "Fighting in front of visitors." Some of the girls looked away. "Go down to the locker rooms," he said. "All of you. There'll be no more cheerleading today. Whatever's wrong, we'll iron it out tomorrow."

The girls backed away, moving in disgruntled and mumbling groups toward the doors of the gym. Mike walked over to Pat. She wanted to put her arms around her, but Pat shook her head. There were tears in her eyes.

"Let me go, Mike," she whispered. "Let me get out of here without bawling."

The buzzer called Mike back to the game. Intermission was over. She stood there watching her sister walking head down toward the locker rooms. Then she turned and crossed the court to her place with her team.

She managed to play the last half. It was only because of her instinctive feel for the game that she was able to stay with it. She saw the ball come to her, smelled the leather, felt the sting of it on her hands, watched it loop through the air as she passed it or shot for the basket. She heard the screams from the stands, the Greenport rooters cheering their team. The Westbrook side was strangely quiet. It seemed almost as if they had caught some of the shame that had sent their cheerleaders in disgrace from the gym floor.

Mike played the game but she was not with it. Her mind was elsewhere, down in the locker room where Pat, alone, sobbing, a little frightened at what she had unwittingly become caught up in, was braving it out.

Mike heard a laugh and she came suddenly awake. She glanced across the court where Emma was holding forth. The stands were roaring at her antics.

Let her show off, Mike thought. This is her game. She got what she wanted.

Although a half-dozen times Mike wanted to scream to Miss Yates to take her off the court, she stayed. She didn't go out. She made a basket whenever she found the ball in her hands and the basket clear before her. But her heart wasn't in it. Her heart, like her mind, was down in the locker room with Pat.

When the buzzer finally sounded she felt only relief. She had to get to her sister. Without waiting for the final cheer for Greenport, she ran across the floor toward the open door.

On the way a chance sentence from someone in the stands slowed her up, but only for a moment.

"Hey, what are you running away from, Patterson?" a voice called. "Afraid to face the music? Take a look at the scoreboard."

She did, turning back for just a second in her pell-mell flight toward the exit.

Visitors, 40; Westbrook, 21.

"Nice going," the same sarcastic voice followed her. "Nice going, Mike. Keep that up and they'll hand you a lemon instead of a silver loving cup." Several voices joined in the laugh that followed. Mike didn't look back. She didn't care about anything but Pat.

TEN

THE REPERCUSSIONS of the Westbrook-Greenport game were numerous.

The Westbrook cheerleaders and the basketball team were called into Mr. Davis's office for a dressing down.

"I'm not pinning the blame on any one person," Mr. Davis said. "I suspect the girls' basketball team was as much at fault as the cheerleading squad. However I don't like squabbles in sports activities. Interschool sports are supposed to foster good will. It's fine to want to beat the other fellow, fairly and squarely, but there's no room for personal animosities." He permitted a bit of humor to creep into his lecture, saying that he always understood that the female was more deadly than the male when roused to anger and that after the public exhibition of the other afternoon he was convinced.

"Now, girls," he finished. "Or should I say, ladies, I hope we'll never be treated to another such performance. No matter what happens, keep personal quarrels out of sports!"

That was all. Mr. Davis's kind of discipline was the toughest to take. He didn't bellow or dole out penalties. He just talked in that quiet way of his, looking them straight in the eye by turns and making them feel cheap.

Miss Yates had her turn. She was not so soft-spoken as Mr. Davis and she was a lot more angry. She was a woman who insisted on facing facts. The facts were obvious in this case. The basketball team had been permitting personal rivalry to break up its teamwork. That in itself was bad enough. But to spread the quarrel to the cheerleaders, stir up strife in another organization, was petty and mean. It could give girls' sports a very bad name. Women, she pointed out, had been fighting hard for a long time to get equal rights in many fields. Some people still thought that women weren't capable of handling themselves as well as men, that women were emotionally unstable. The sort of thing that had been going on in the Westbrook basketball team was not convincing proof that women had a right to the privileges they had fought so hard to get.

When Miss Yates finished, you could have heard a pin drop in the room. She asked if anyone wanted to say anything. Not a hand went up. The girls were content to file out of her office in silence.

Mike had her special session with Miss Yates. She was called down during a free period. Miss Yates wanted to talk with Mike about the last half of the Greenport game. Something had happened to Mike's game.

Miss Yates kept pumping Mike until she came out with the facts. Mike told her she just didn't have her heart in the game. Basketball didn't give her the kick it used to, before all this razzle-dazzle surrounded it. Team rivalry was fine but she didn't like this personal competition. You couldn't play good basketball while your mind was on a nasty remark one of your teammates had passed about you and on your sister bawling her eyes out down in the locker room. Mike was careful not to mention Emma Gaudet's name.

"You and Emma don't like each other very well, do you?" Miss Yates asked quietly.

"I like her all right," Mike blurted out. "I don't think she likes me."

"I'll talk with Emma," Miss Yates said.

"I wish you wouldn't, Miss Yates. I mean it will only make things worse. She'll think I talked to you about her. Please let me see if I can straighten it out between us."

"All right," Miss Yates answered. "I'll wait. But I won't wait long, Mike. I don't want my girls tearing each other's hair—or hearts—out." She looked up smiling.

She's nice, Mike thought. She gets your point right away. "Thanks," she said. "Thanks a lot, Miss Yates."

"Mike." Mike turned back. "Mike, don't let personal feelings throw you for a loop. We've all got to learn to take it. We can't expect things to go along evenly. Life rubs us. Jostles and pushes us around. We've got to keep our balance no matter what happens. We can't let a few nasty bumps from the crowd put us out of the running."

The eventful Westbrook-Greenport game had an even wider backlash than a few sound lectures delivered to the girls of Westbrook High. Mike watched it cause a complete reversal in educational tactics. She soon heard that the physical-education teachers of the county had passed a ruling that everything possible should be done to foster amity among those participating in sports, both within the schools and between the schools. They voted to put their resolution into immediate action and the next boys' Westbrook-Brighthaven basketball game would be the testing ground.

Mike could see why the physical-education teachers should choose Westbrook and Brighthaven Highs as their focal point in promoting friendly relations in sports.

The two schools were ancient rivals. Even when Mike had been in grade school, she had heard about the bitter competition between them. It was something everyone took for granted because the schools were such evenly matched rivals.

Both high schools were big, million-dollar buildings with medium-sized enrollments. The classes were not bursting at the seams as were those in so many American high schools. The teaching staff was carefully selected and better paid than elsewhere. The schools "had everything." Nothing new appeared upon the horizon of American education but that Brighthaven and Westbrook immediately gave it a try. They had camera clubs, French clubs, Latin clubs, stamp clubs, coin clubs, short story and journalism and poetry clubs, acting and stagecraft and scene-design clubs, ballet and modern-dancing clubs, clubs to which students belonged in an attempt to find out which other clubs they wished to join.

The cafeterias of both schools were large and spotless. The food—although the students admitted it grudgingly—was good. The auditoriums were large, with murals done by prominent artists, and fully equipped stages that would have put many off-Broadway theaters to shame.

The gymnasium in which Mike had spent so many of her afternoons was modern and faultless. It could be divided in two to form two complete courts where both girls and boys might practice if necessary. The stands were movable; the lighting and sports equipment, perfect.

The young people who arrived daily at the portals of these two ducational institutions came, as do high-school students everywhere, on bicycles, in jalopies, in convertibles. Some were disgorged from yellow buses or from family cars driven by harassed mothers who spelled each other in the chore. Some even walked.

They were, for the most part, healthy, American boys and girls, well dressed and well fed, with the most important worries on their minds whether they could get their Latin or trig or history finished before the last bell; whether, if they were boys, they would have enough cash in their pockets for the big date on Friday, or, if they were girls, whether their particular Joe or Tom or Jim would ask them to the next dance.

They kidded and joked, they were quiet at times, they griped endlessly about everything without meaning it. They had high hopes for themselves. They suffered endlessly, as only the young can suffer, but they were sure that within themselves they held the answer to everything.

Mike was one of these. She belonged to her world, and her world was compassed by what she had experienced, by what she knew to be true. She was like all people who read a great deal, a challenger of the printed word, trusting only what she felt sure was the truth. She was sure of one thing, that she belonged to Westbrook and, in a narrower sense, to Westbrook High School.

So when Mike learned that Westbrook was to join Brighthaven in what the students ironically referred to as the "Big Diplomatic Shindig," she felt, with good reason, a vague uneasiness.

The "Big Diplomatic Shindig" was being elaborately prepared for by the faculties of both schools. It would consist of a basketball game between the boys of Westbrook and Brighthaven, played at the latter school. After the game, there would be a "Tramp Dance" in the Brighthaven gym. Refreshments would be served. Everyone was welcome.

The night of the affair, Mike was picked up at six-thirty by Shirl and Deedie. Pat was going over on a special bus with the cheerleaders.

When they reached Brighthaven, the high-school parking lot was almost filled with cars but they managed to find a spot. They entered the building to discover the place was already a madhouse. The gym was roaring with cheers for Brighthaven.

Mike kept her eyes open as she and her friends threaded their way to the gym. It had been several days since she had seen Jeff. He had telephoned but had not asked for a date. He used an injury sustained during a skiing jaunt as an excuse, explaining he had been hobbling around for a few days.

She thought of course that he wouldn't be able to play basketball tonight. That must be a hard thing for him to take, being captain of the Brighthaven team. But he would surely turn out for the game and she watched for him.

When she sat down on the Westbrook side of the gymnasium, she was surprised to see Jeff out on the court, dressed in his uniform, running toward the basket, and tossing in a banked shot.

He looks perfectly sound of limb to me! she thought. I wonder if he really. . . .

Before the thought was finished, she had to move over for a couple of Westbrook boys.

"Hey," one of the boys called to his chum. "Look, Parker's playing tonight. I thought he was out of the game."

"He was," the other boy replied. "Got an O.K. from his doctor this afternoon. He's all right if he takes it easy."

"That guy take it easy!" The first boy laughed. "Not a chance. He plays like a maniac."

"We should worry," the second boy retorted. "If he gets carried out, it's Brighthaven's funeral."

The game started promptly at seven-fifteen. It was like all boys' games, fast and rough, with the points piled up on both sides with dizzying speed. Mike was sitting in the second row of the stands where she had a good view of Jeff. She could not take her eyes off him. She found herself pulled between loyalty to Westbrook and her fondness for Jeff. When Westbrook made a basket, she let out a yowl of triumph, but when Jeff made a basket for Brighthaven, she wanted to shout "Yippee! Nice going, Jeff!" She couldn't. She had to clamp her jaws shut.

He had what it takes to make a first-class player. He was fast, smart, with terrific control, an unfailing eye for the basket, but he had that something extra too, that thing called style.

Twice he came down hard on his weak ankle and Mike who was watching him more closely than anyone else could see him lurch. She gasped, feeling for him, but he went on playing.

At the end of the half, the score was Brighthaven, twenty-four; Westbrook, twenty. Mike couldn't make up her mind whom she wanted to win.

The last half of the game was rougher. Everything was stepped up, the dribbling, the pace, the shooting. In a game as close as this, the playing was bound to get out of hand. Mike noticed plenty of elbowing and kneeing, even shoving. It was hard for the two officials to check all of it. Mike worried about Jeff. With that bad ankle, he was a perfect target for an injury.

It was during the last quarter with the score a tie, both schools having made thirty-three points, that it happened.

Jeff was playing close to the basket, waiting for a recovery. The ball teetered on the rim as one of his teammates missed a shot. Jeff caught it, poised for a shot. A banked shot might have done it, Mike thought, and she hoped Jeff would try for one. He didn't. He used a pivot shot, expecting to get it clean through the basket. As he swung around, he came down too hard on his weak ankle. The ball tumbled from his hands and he sprawled on the floor. Mike jumped to her feet, stifling the scream in her throat.

Jeff was up. He tried to walk, but could only stagger across the floor, lurching like a wounded animal. Mike put

84

her hand to her throat, wanting to shout out to him to stop.

"He's hurt!" Mike caught snatches of the screaming around her. Both Westbrook and Brighthaven rooters were on their feet.

The floor space around Jeff cleared as the Brighthaven coach and the school doctor bent over to examine his leg. There was talk about a stretcher but Jeff waved them off. Mike was close enough to see the pain on his face. She felt it herself, felt it for him.

I don't want him hurt, she thought. I don't want anything to happen to him.

She wanted to run out on the court, to jump down over the row of people on the bench in front of her and race across the floor to Jeff. She couldn't do it. She was Mike Patterson of Westbrook. She would make a laughing-stock of herself if she ran out there.

Then someone else did what Mike wanted to do. Before the officials had time to put their arms around Jeff and help him off the floor, a figure from the Brighthaven side darted out. It was a girl, a tall girl in a plaid skirt and a white sweater. She rushed to Jeff's side as they led him off the court.

The stands began to cheer, both schools joining in.

Mike watched Jeff. The girl walked beside him, tried to hold his hand but he pulled away.

As the cheering quieted down, Mike heard the boy next to her talking to his chum.

"Who's the doll?" he asked.

"She's a doll, that's for sure," the other boy answered. "Charleen Morgan. Goes to Miss Covington's school. She's Parker's one and only."

"Yeah? I wouldn't mind getting hurt real bad if a girl like that would try to hold my hand." The boys laughed. "Say, I thought he was dating someone at Westbrook. Didn't I hear . . . ?"

"Ssssh!" The other boy hushed him, glancing at Mike. He pulled his friend closer and whispered in his ear.

The first boy hunched his shoulders, pulling up his collar in embarrassment. "Ouch!" he said. "Why doesn't someone tell me these things. Me and my big mouth."

The game went on. Mike watched it through blurred eyes. It didn't matter now that Westbrook shot ahead of Brighthaven. It didn't matter that the final score was forty-nine to thirty-nine in favor of her own school. All that mattered was the picture that was stamped indelibly on her consciousness. The picture of a tall girl in a plaid skirt and a white sweater, a girl who had the nerve to dash across the basketball court to Jeff's side.

She's a doll, that's for sure. She's Parker's one and only.

ELEVEN

MIKE WAS going to the V.I.P. dance. She had to keep stating this fact over and over in order to convince herself that it was true. Two months, even six weeks ago, the dance which the V.I.P. club gave on Valentine's Day every year seemed a part of a world to which Mike would never belong.

"Everyone will wear color," Pat said when they chose this dress. "There's nothing more outstanding than a tall girl in a slim midnight-blue dress that really fits her. It's glamorous!"

But she was going, no mistake about it. In her closet hung the dress she had bought for the occasion. Pat had helped her select it. It was midnight blue, slim, well-fitting.

It was glamorous, all right. Mike daydreamed constantly about the dress. As she sat through classes, had lunch in the cafeteria, chatted with friends, or bounced the basketball around the gym, the dress would loom up before her. There she was, slim and tall and attractive in midnight blue, with the three-strand pearl necklace from Pat's jewel box making her long neck seem less like a crane's, her mother's pearl and rhinestone spray earrings, and demi-heeled shoes that gave her an elegant high-heeled look without adding three inches to her height.

"Be proud of your height," Pat kept dinning. "It's nothing to be ashamed of. And if I ever see you trying to scrunch down, making yourself stoop-shouldered to appear shorter, Mike, so help me, I'll kick you in the shins."

Mike laughed. She had no intention of drooping at the shoulders. She liked being tall, so long as the boy who was taking her was several inches taller and Red Goodrich was all of that. He towered at a stunning six-feet-one and one-half inches.

She was not going with Jeff, and this was the one cloud on a horizon that was bright with the prospect of the Sweetheart Dance. Jeff was taking Charleen. It was an open secret shared by the student bodies of Westbrook and Brighthaven, Greenport and Brampton and New Sharon. Every school in the county was informed to the hilt about the V.I.P. affair.

Small as it was, with only twenty boys and their girls, it was an easy matter to count on your fingers who was going with whom. Since the V.I.P. boys chose their girls from a wide radius, every school in the county would be represented at the dance.

It was interesting how Mike had come to be one of the favored twenty girls invited.

Pat was going with Al Goodrich who was alternately known as "Lefty," "Southpaw," "Bulldozer," and "Alfonzo." Al had a cousin named Red about whom he lamented one evening to Pat while they were having their third malted in Al's car, parked in front of the Dairy Queen.

Red was a wonderful guy, the best, a very good egg. He played tackle on the Brighthaven football team. He read books. He was an amateur photographer of some repute. He was huge, handsome in a ruddy way, but he had freckles and a shock of bright red hair that almost blinded the casual observer. Al, who fancied himself as something of a psychologist, had this redheaded cousin of his figured out. He was scared stiff of girls and he was sensitive.

"Got a regular complex about that carrot-thatch of his." Al nodded, tossing away his straw and gulping down the last half of his malted. "Thinks everyone is always laughing about it, noticing it, and passing remarks. Heck, maybe they are, but that's no reason to shut himself up like a hermit in a cave. He's got to come out of his shell. I keep telling him to make a play for some nice girl. Two or three of them. 'You'll see, Red,' I keep telling him. 'Once you break the ice, it's a cinch. They'll flock around you like bees around honey.' I just keep telling him."

Pat was sympathetic. She understood perfectly. She had

a sister Mike who had been that way about boys. Recently her sister had come out of her shell a bit, but the job was by no means done. She had fallen head over heels for Jeff Parker at Brighthaven who was all snarled up with Charleen Morgan. Mike had been at the Brighthaven-Westbrook boys' game the night Charleen had run out on the floor. Mike was still nursing her wounds. It was a shame. It was, indeed, a minor tragedy.

Girls or boys who couldn't get their romantic lives straightened out were in a sad way. Both Al and Pat philosophized at length on the subject, agreeing that it was up to better-adjusted friends and relatives to help them out.

The upshot of their discussion was a telephone call from Red Goodrich to Mike Patterson asking her, between coughs and long pauses, if she would like to go to the V.I.P. dance with him. Mike had been primed for the call. She was prepared for the reticence on the other end of the wire. She had also been lectured to, wheedled, cajoled, begged, threatened, and pleaded with. Pat had done a thorough job of preparation. Mike said yes, she'd be glad to go with Red. Red coughed again, stammered something Mike couldn't understand, and hung up.

The important thing was that she had been asked, that she had accepted, that she would be there. Jeff and Charleen Morgan would be there too, and Mike might find out how much they really meant to each other.

In the evening of Valentine's Day, Mike and Pat and the Goodrich boys drove in Red's car to the Longshore Club where the party was being given. Mike was grateful that Red had to tend to his driving because in the few moments of introduction he had seemed painfully self-conscious. She wondered what on earth they would talk about if he ever got to the point of uttering one continuous sentence, uninterrupted by coughs or pauses.

She had had a fleeting glimpse of his hair. It was the most violent red hair she had ever seen, and even a crewcut only seemed to emphasize its prominence. Mike's first impulse was to blink and then break into a long, slow smile. She had done neither. Her long years spent in the shadow of an adored and beautiful sister had taught her this much: to understand the unhappiness of another.

She did not stop with Red's hair, but had let her eyes wander down the whole long, powerful frame of the boy. She had noted the huge shoulders, the easy, athletic grace, the strong features, much more handsome than Pat or Al had depicted them. She had been aware too of deeper things, of a kind of gentleness which sometimes showed itself surprisingly in big and powerful males, and she sensed too the intelligence of the boy before her.

In his dinner jacket worn for the occasion, he made a fine figure of a man and Mike, without revealing it, felt proud to be with him.

The hair is a bit overwhelming, she thought, but the rest is nice. Wonderfully, unbelievably nice and I'm glad of that.

Although Mike had never been to the Longshore Club, Pat had been there many times, so Mike stuck close to her sister while they left their wraps with a smiling Negro man in a white coat, then went upstairs to comb their hair.

Mike recognized only two other girls in the crowded powder room, a Brighthaven basketball player and a senior from Westbrook. She felt quiet in the presence of all these girls. The mirror told her that she did not look so different from the rest of them, taller than most perhaps, with not so much make-up, yet she did not *feel* like one of them. They seemed at ease, as if they were used to getting into a formal gown every night and going to parties. They wore their clothes with an air, and Mike knew, beyond all cavil, that she was not wearing her midnight-blue dress with an air. It made her feel self-conscious because it was cut low, and the skirt was long and narrow and slit at the bottom. The choker of pearls felt tight at her throat and she longed for the soft comfort of her old, flat-heeled shoes.

More even than the manner in which they carried their clothes was a kind of comradeship that existed among these girls. They followed a pattern in their conversation which seemed a little shallow to her. They chatted endlessly about nothing. Then she realized it was not just "nothing" they were talking about, but concrete things in which she had no genuine interest—perfumes, a jeweled bracelet, a pair of earrings, the cut of a dress, a gilt compact. They talked about their "men" in a strange patronizing way, and Mike had not yet been initiated into this female society. She would be glad when it was time to go downstairs.

For one brief moment, she felt her heart leap and her tongue stick to the roof of her mouth. It was when Charleen Morgan entered the powder room. She came in late, after most of the other girls had finished primping. Everyone in the room turned to look at her. Mike would have recognized her, even if a chorus of "Hi, Charleen" had not greeted her entrance. She was the kind of girl whom, having seen once, you did not readily forget.

Tonight she looked very different from the girl who on the evening of the basketball game had rushed across the floor in a plaid skirt and white sweater. Her dress was satin, a shade of green with so much yellow in it that it appeared almost golden. It was the longest and fullest dress in the room. Charleen's perfect shoulders rose above the yellow-green. She wore no necklace, but a golden halter was draped around the neckline of the dress and her gold filigree earrings touched her shoulders. One arm was covered halfway to the elbow with gold bracelets, and a golden rose was pinned in her hair.

The silence that fell over the room as the girls studied Charleen's costume, bit by bit, was mute tribute to its distinction.

Pat pulled Mike toward the door but Mike hung back long enough to see this girl in action. Charleen was no tongue-tied clotheshorse. Her conversation was lively. She became at once the center of an animated discussion.

Mike grabbed Pat at the top of the stairs. "Whew!" she exclaimed. "How could I ever expect to make the grade with Jeff when he's got something like that?"

"Don't talk about yourself that way," Pat said sharply. "And don't be bowled over by the green satin dress."

"Maybe if I'd bought a dress like that, Jeff might have noticed me."

91

"It's not your type," Pat said firmly. "Your dress is perfect for you." She shook her head. "Forget Jeff. You didn't come to be noticed by him. You came to have a good time. With Red. Remember?"

Mike grinned at Pat. "Yes, Mamma," she whispered.

"Don't give Jeff the first dance he asks for." Pat frowned. "Don't give him even the second dance he asks for. Make him run after you."

"Do you think he will? With a girl like Charleen he won't even notice me."

"He'll notice you," Pat said, tossing her head in confidence.

The ballroom of the club was handsomely decorated for the occasion. The V.I.P.'s had used the "comic valentine" theme for their dance. Around the room were cartoons, poster-style, done by one of the boys, depicting comic characters: a miser, a spinster, a vamp, a milktoast character, a shrew. At one end was a table with plates and cups and silverware, ready for the buffet supper that would be served later on. Two waiters in Gay Nineties costumes were getting ready to serve punch.

As Red handed Mike her dance program, he nodded toward the posters, "Any resemblance to any character living or dead is strictly intentional."

Mike, surprised at the quip, nodded toward the typical spinster cartoon, bun at the back of her head, high shoes, stern face. "Sometimes I think I'll wind up like that."

Red laughed a good laugh, deep and hearty. "As long as we have our hair down, I might as well confess." He pointed to the milktoast character. "That 's me. The minute I see an attractive girl like you I want to run."

"Thanks," Mike said. "I feel better already." She glanced out at the dance floor where a few couples had begun to dance. "Now that we've been introduced," she said, "maybe we could try dancing together."

Red held out his arms. "I'm going to like you," he said. "You say what you think. You're my kind of girl." He held her off and looked at her. "Hey," he went on. "That's the first time I've ever talked like that to a girl." He seemed pleased with himself. "Maybe I'm not doing so bad."

It was a fine party. Mike who had felt so out of place in the stuffiness of the powder room lost her timidity and had the best time she had ever had in her life. She danced with every good friend of Red's and there were many.

When Red caught up with her again on the fifth dance, he said, "Well, it's about time. I'd begun to think I was losing you. I don't want that to happen."

She found out a lot about Red in the two dances that followed and while they were eating supper. He liked to read as much as she did. He liked to take long walks too. They had both explored Hunter Hill, the Mad River Grove, Fisherman's Rest, all the solitary places in the county that an inveterate hiker might ferret out.

"If I tell you something," he said, "promise you won't laugh."

"I won't," Mike replied.

"When Al told me to call you for a date, I was glad."

"You were?"

He nodded. "I've watched you play basketball. Been to some of the girls' games this year. You're tops. I just sit there screaming my head off for you when you make a basket. I think to myself, if I ever get a girl, that's the kind of girl she's going to be. A girl with fight." Red grew suddenly quiet. "I don't know why I talk to you like this," he said. "I guess you think I'm a screwball to talk like that."

"I don't think any such thing," she said. "I think you're swell."

"You do?" He beamed. "You honestly mean that, Mike?"

"I honestly mean it."

Mike had wondered all evening what she would do if she came face to face with Jeff. She was conscious of him, of course, painfully conscious of him floating always on the edge of the crowd, dancing off into corners with Charleen Morgan. They seemed to keep to themselves. Mike wondered who was at fault. Was it Jeff who wanted Charleen all to himself or vice versa?

Once Jeff asked Red for a dance with Mike, but Red

turned him down, saying, "This girl of mine is too popular. I can't get enough dances myself."

Jeff looked disappointed and Mike was secretly glad that Red had taken over the problem of turning him down. Despite Pat's warning, she would never have been able to refuse Jeff.

Now Jeff came across to where Red and Mike were sitting, their buffet plates on their laps.

"Hello, stranger," he said to Mike. "Do I get that dance?" Mike looked at Red who pulled out her program.

"Let's see," Red drawled. "She's got the next one with me, then after that, one with Tony Ruta, then one with Sam Camp, then. . . ."

Jeff cut in. "Never mind whom she's got them with. Just tell me what one I can have."

Red stared wide-eyed at Jeff. "Now, now, there's no use getting excited," he said. "Just about a little old dance."

"A little old dance!" Jeff repeated. "Mike is my best friend and I've got a right to have one dance with her at least."

"Your best friend!" Red sounded amazed, and Mike suspected that he was a pretty good actor. "Why, I thought you brought the girl over there, the one in the green dress and all the gilt. What's her name, Charlotte, Cherie?" Red snapped his fingers.

Mike had never seen Jeff angry before. "Never mind her name," he said. "Mike's a good friend of mine, and I want a dance with her."

Red stood up. He carefully set down his plate. He looked Jeff up and down and then he said, "Jeff, if Mike's your best friend, why didn't you bring her to the dance?" Jeff colored, looking away. "If you want to dance with Mike, you'll have to wait until the 'Deuce's Wild' dance when you can cut in all you please. Mike's booked solid otherwise. So please be a good boy and go away and let us alone."

Jeff turned away without a word.

Mike and Red watched him walk back to Charleen. "Jeff's a good guy, but he's got one big fault," Red commented. "He wants his own way and he's used to getting it."

They stopped talking about Jeff. Yet Mike could not stop thinking about him and Red's remark. She wondered if Red was right. Mike had never thought of it before. Maybe Jeff was spoiled. He always got his way about everything. She wasn't sure but that might be the trouble.

He cut in on her during the "Deuce's Wild" dance as Red had suggested he do. He was the first one to grab her when the whistle blew to change partners and he whisked her off the floor as fast as he could before the whistle could blow again.

"You shouldn't do this," she said as he led her into one of the anterooms off the main ballroom and continued to whirl her around to the music.

"It's the only way I can get you alone, Mike."

Jeff did all the talking. He told Mike how much he had missed her and how sorry he was that his skiing accident had kept him laid up.

"I had hoped to see you at the Tramp Dance, Mike," he finished. "But I didn't stay for it."

"Yes, I know," she told him. "I was at the game." He looked away. "I see your foot is much better," she went on. "I'm glad of that."

The music swung suddenly into the Latin rhythm of the mambo. As they danced around the room, Jeff asked, "Remember the night you learned the mambo?"

"I remember," she said. She glanced at the silver skier dangling from her wrist and Jeff's eyes followed hers. Neither one of them spoke of what was most in their thoughts—Charleen Morgan.

Jeff was the first to break their silence. "You're so quiet tonight, Mike. Aren't you having a good time?"

"I've been having a perfectly wonderful time," she said.

"You mean until now."

"I didn't say that."

"But you implied it. You'd been having a good time until I barged in. I wish it were the opposite, Mike. I wish you would have said you'd been having a miserable time until now, until we danced together."

"That wouldn't be the truth. Red's a lot of fun."

"I would have liked it if you could have told me that you'd rather have been here with me."

"What good would that do? To wish for a thing like that. You evidently wanted to bring someone else."

"I didn't want it at all. I'd much rather have brought you, Mike. But this was a date made long before we met each other."

"How could that be?" she asked him, pointedly. "I thought that you joined up with V.I.P. and me at the same time. Or have you forgotten how we met each other?"

"I wish you'd forget that silly business. You know how I feel about that." He pulled her toward him, making her look into his eyes. "You know how badly I feel about that, Mike. Say you do. Tell me you know."

"Maybe," she said. "Maybe I do."

"I made this date with Charleen weeks before I joined V.I.P. I foolishly promised her I'd take her to every school dance this year. I can see now it was wrong, but you wouldn't want me to break a promise, would you?"

"She certainly knows how to tie a boy up for good, doesn't she?" she replied.

"I wish you could understand about Charleen and me, Mike."

"I understand," she flared back. "I think I understand very well."

Jeff was stammering, half apologizing. "Charleen's not like you. She's not your kind of girl. She's different. She needs understanding. Lots of it."

She stopped dancing and broke away from him. "I don't think I like this conversation, Jeff. Not one single bit."

"Don't go away mad, Mike." He reached for her arm. "Let's have a date soon. Let's talk everything over." He held her fast with one hand and with the other he reached for the arm that held the bracelet from which his silver skier dangled.

"You can't be so awfully mad at me," he said, holding on to the skier. "You're still wearing this." He pulled her toward him, with her head close to his, he leaned his cheek against hers, whispering, "I'm glad you're wearing it, Mike. Wear it always. It means a lot to me. It honestly does. I've never given anything like that to another girl." He let go of her arm and held her face between his hands.

"Mike, when I said I missed you, I meant it. I couldn't get you out of my mind. I need you, Mike. You're the only girl I've ever talked to like this. Believe me, Mike. You've got to believe me." She did not pull away this time and he kissed her, full on the mouth, a long kiss which she returned.

Into their kiss there broke the sharp, strident laugh of another girl. Then a husky voice. "Why, Jeff, I had no idea you were here." Mike broke away from Jeff and faced the door. Charleen, flanked by a blond boy and another couple, stood there.

It was to Jeff she spoke but it was Mike who drew her scornful glance as she went on.

"Jeff, we've been looking everywhere for you. Why didn't you tell me that you had unfinished business? I had no idea you were still performing part of your initiation assignment into V.I.P."

The words were cutting. They were spoken with cruel calculation that showed in the toss of Charleen's head, the arrogant droop of her mouth. There was no doubt as to the intention of Charleen's remark. She wanted to squelch Mike once and for all. With the same ruthlessness with which she had bound Jeff to her, she intended to push this interfering girl away from them.

Mike boiled. Everything inside her churned at Charleen's brutal sarcasm. With her anger was mingled the humiliation of a public scene. Others were there to hear Charleen, to go and tell the cruel accusation Charleen had made.

Mike waited. She expected Jeff to speak up to this girl. An angry, "Charleen!" broke from his lips, but that was not enough. That was only a warning. It was certainly not a defense of Mike.

Mike turned and ran blindly from the room, out into the hall. She could not see, she could only feel. What she felt was complete betrayal. Jeff who had kissed her so tenderly and spoken to her so ardently just a moment before had not risen to her defense.

She hurried along the hall until someone reached out and caught her. She looked up into Red Goodrich's face. "Where do you think you're going?" he asked.

He drew her toward him and for the second time that evening she leaned against a boy, only this time it was for comfort. She, a girl who almost never cried, leaned against Red Goodrich in a corner of the corridor of the Longshore Club and sobbed.

She told him everything. Red was a boy you could talk to and she desperately needed someone like him now, someone who listened well and did not interrupt.

They went back and joined the rest of the party. Mike was herself again, smiling, serene. At least so she appeared to the rest of the dancers. She waved to Pat across the floor. She chatted with Red. She was careful not to glance over toward the green satin dress at the far end of the ballroom, but she was aware of it swishing around in the corner that Jeff and Charleen seemed to have reserved for themselves.

Hog-tied, she thought. I suspected it from the beginning and now I'm sure. Maybe it's partly my fault. Maybe I've been too good a sport.

She's not your kind of girl.

That's my trouble, Mike thought. I'm the wrong kind of girl. Just a good egg, just somebody's sister. Maybe what I ought to do is change myself, not Jeff. Maybe that's the real trouble.

From now on I'm going to be different too!

TWELVE

MIKE WAS as good as her word, even though that word had been merely a promise to herself as she watched Jeff and Charleen at the Longshore Club.

"I've been the good-sport type too long," she told Pat. "From now on, everything's going to be different."

Pat had always said, from the time they had been kids in playsuits and pigtails that when Mike *really* made up her mind, there was no stopping her.

So, with grim determination, Mike concentrated on becoming what she was not. She took some lessons in her own home, watching and listening to Pat. She learned that there were ways of looking at a boy, ways of talking to a boy. There were ways to walk, to toss your head, to look up into a boy's eyes. There were times to talk, and times to keep still. There was a special art in greeting a boy, in the inflection you gave his name, in the way you talked to him over the telephone, in the way you said, "Good-by."

All these things had been happening right under Mike's nose for years, but she had paid no attention. Now she observed, and practiced her observations on the boys who began in increasing numbers to seek her out. It was no longer a sure thing when the telephone rang in the Patterson house that the call was for Pat. Almost as frequently these days, it was for Mike.

Mike did not confine her research to the precincts of her own home. She went abroad, so to speak, and kept her eyes open. In classrooms, in the assembly hall, in the cafeteria, on the walks and terraces and parking lot of the sprawling school building, in the public library, in bean wagons and restaurants, in the high-school room at the Y, in short, wherever girl meets boy and sets to work on him, Mike watched and learned.

The results were phenomenal. Pat said so, her brothers home for a midsemester breather said so, her girl friends said so. The boys of her acquaintance did not say anything. They were too stunned by the emotional impact of an exciting new girl in their midst.

That girl was Mike Patterson.

It was not just enough that she learned how to put on lipstick without Pat's help. Or that she let her hair grow to a becoming length and trained it to fall in soft waves. Or that she discovered she had a skin which, with proper care, would bring comments from schoolmates about its fine texture.

It was not even enough that she learned how to dress, not dress *up*, which was something else again, but to dress beautifully every time she put on clothes.

This began as a chore, but she soon discovered that it could be exciting fun. Always an intense person, she brought this intensity to her new interest in clothes. She did it by singling out the four girls at school whom she considered the best dressed and studying them, exhaustively, every day of their lives without their knowing it. She was clever enough not to copy them, but to develop a style of her own. Christmas and birthday money that was lying in an envelope marked "Mike" in the family strongbox came out into the open. She had accumulated a tidy sum because she "just never seemed to want anything." Now she wanted with a vengeance.

She learned, with Pat at her elbow, and her eyes and ears wide open to the comments of salesclerks, the difference between cheap and fine materials, clothes that were well made and those that were not, clothes that fit and those which hung like potato sacks. She learned the feel of a cashmere sweater, the smell of good leather, the simple elegance of a dress that was all line. She learned to rip off gewgaws, rhinestone buckles and bows and pearl ornaments. She found out how to stand before a mirror and be merciless about herself, to decide with swift and dispassionate taste what was suitable to her figure and her height and her coloring, and what was not.

She caught the knack of individualizing herself and, somewhere along the line, she became aware that style was a kind of beauty available to all.

Plain colors, stark simplicity, a choker of silver beads, a bright splash of color in a Chinese gold or chartreuse scarf, these were part of the casual sophistication she strove to attain.

It did not come easily to her, although much of her development was interesting if only because she was venturing into new and untried fields. She labored over this new self the way a butterfly must push and work its way from its chrysalis. It was accomplished only with persistence and patience and some sacrifice of the rough shell in which she had so long encased herself.

She had to emerge into a new world, a world unknown in many ways, and in some ways hostile, an untried world of which she was somewhat afraid. Until now she had been big, booming Mike Patterson who was half child and whose chief concept of competition was to lick the stuffing out of a rival team on a basketball court.

She learned that there is a wider competition in the world, the competition a girl accepts when she takes her place among other women. Now she had to hold her own as a woman, not just a kid dribbling a basketball or heaving a hook shot through a metal rim.

That was why all these external things were not enough.

There was more to be done, much more, before she would be the kind of person she had determined to become. Even her new clothes did not give her the self-assurance she wanted. They helped, but much of the groundwork for this new self had to be built within, in flashes of insight into the handling of other people. She had always been direct, spilling out whatever she had to say. She became more tactful. She could never quite bring herself to adopt a "line" as so many of the girls did, saying things they did not mean, but she did learn to keep silence instead of striking out right and left with her opinions, wounding egos all along the way.

It was remarkable what you could do in four or five weeks when you set your mind to it. It was the motive behind every act that counted, and the motive behind Mike's transformation was to be the kind of girl Jeff had insinuated she was not, smooth, sophisticated, a little worldly-wise, self-assured and idolized, as Jeff apparently idolized Charleen Morgan.

She especially wanted to be adored, not just by one boy now, as she had wanted to be a few short months ago, because she knew that to be impossible. That boy was hogtied by a glamour girl with gold bracelets halfway up her arm. Not being able to command his attention, she determined to be sought after by many boys.

She was indeed.

It seemed to be mostly a matter of setting her mind to it. This was a remarkable bit of enlightenment for Mike. It had never occurred to her that being an attractive girl was something to be learned and practiced and mastered in much the way she had learned to shoot a goal in basketball.

She entered upon a new life. She did not neglect her studies or basketball. Because of her remarkable energy, she was able to go on with her former interests and still follow the pattern she had laid out for herself. She made a few rules and these she held to with adamant strength of will. She would date only on Friday and Saturday nights. She would maintain her good grades and keep in training so her basketball form would not be impaired. She would never accept any date that she felt to be an utter waste of time.

Pat laughed at her.

"You're the limit," she said. "You organize your life as if you were Secretary of State or something."

Among the two most persistent boys who hounded Mike these days were Flash Feeney and Red Goodrich. Flash had always been a hanger-on at the Patterson house, trailing on the outskirts of Pat's long list of friends. Now he developed a crush on Mike. Flash was brilliant, unpredictable, and merry. She would look over to the stands during a basketball practice and catch sight of Flash breezing in, yanking off his yellow scarf and gloves, pushing his battered reporter's hat back on his head, and finally jamming it into his pocket.

"Hi, Mike!" he'd yell, waving to her. "Button this game up fast so we can grab some chow."

Everyone laughed at Flash. Everyone liked him and, strangely enough, in the days to follow Mike became known as "Flash's girl." It amused her because the friendship between them was a rollicking platonic one. Flash was shorter than she by one or two inches. He was good-looking enough, with his everlasting smile and fine dark eyes and ruddy complexion, but a romance with Flash was unthinkable.

It was true they went everywhere together, and by being with the ubiquitous Flash, Mike gained in prestige. Flash was fun. There was no use denying that she enjoyed every minute they spent together. His repartee and Celtic wit fascinated Mike. She had never before known a boy who could talk so glibly about almost any subject in the world.

He pin-pointed people with that shrewd intellect of his and analyzed them right down to their funnybones. It amused Mike. It entertained her enormously and she accepted the fact which Flash never doubted for a moment, that one day he would be a successful writer. But she never felt in Flash's fascinating presence, that emotional pull she had always felt when she merely thought about Jeff. When Flash was not with her, she forgot him.

Her relationship with Red was somewhat different. It went deeper, but even so it was not love.

They took long walks together. They went skating. Once they went up to Rolling Giant and Mike's eyes searched the slopes futilely for Jeff, while she remembered the day they had gone over the trail.

In the bean wagon later on, while Red and she were eating hamburgers and listening to the juke box, she kept remembering that day with Jeff. That had been the night he had given her the silver skier. Her eyes went to it now, even while Red was talking to her.

She heard the words, "Mike, I've asked you the same question three times. What's the matter?"

"I'm sorry," she stammered her apology. "I was daydreaming I guess." She pulled her glance away from the silver skier. "What question?"

"Where did you learn that special kind of turn you used this afternoon? I've never seen any other skier use it. It's terrific."

She smiled and a warm glow came over her as she answered. "I worked it out myself one day while I was skiing over the trail."

"Over the trail!" Red exclaimed. "Say, I didn't know you were that good."

She patted his sleeve. "It's a long story. Sometime I'll tell you about it."

Red looked confused, as if she had somehow passed him by. That was always the trouble, no matter whom she was with. She got a big bang out of Flash and she liked Red, liked him with an affection that was compounded of respect and mutual interests and the kind of fondness you were bound to feel for a boy who treated you with so much consideration. Yet, hovering always in the background, no matter where she was, no matter what she was doing, was the memory of the few times she had been out with Jeff.

She could not forget him even though she would not date him again. This much she promised herself. Although he telephoned and wanted to see her, she evaded him. By now she had got the pitch. She knew that she could never really have Jeff. If she saw him again, it would only be prolonging the agony.

He belonged with Charleen. A girl who went to Miss Covington's School, who rode horseback and could ski with Jeff without dumping herself head first into the mountainside, who was formidably poised and had money and the assurance that comes from always getting everything you want. Even Jeff. She had wanted Jeff and got him.

Yet while she avoided seeing Jeff, Mike could not put him from her mind. He was always with her. The more

104

she told herself that she must forget him, the more convinced she became that she never would.

As for Jeff, he was having troubles of his own. When he had been as young as his brother Jim, he had understood all he believed there was to understand about women. In general he considered them fuzzy-headed, silly, vain, unreasonable, and gold diggers. All except his mother and Webbsie, of course. These latter were the exceptions that proved his rule.

"Females!" he was then accustomed to snort in disgust. "Females!" And with that one expletive he summed up the sex he felt to be so vastly inferior to his own.

If anyone were now to remind him of this phase through which he had gone, he would have stared back in genuine surprise. He had done a complete reversal on his former stand. So much so that he could not even remember it.

Women, or girls, if you will, he now felt to be rather a bit ahead of boys in shrewdness and cleverness, if not in actual physical skill. The weaker sex still appeared vain and sometimes unreasonable, but they were hardly stupid or fuzzy-headed. They were very often charming and quite delicious, and even their unpredictability he found to be fascinating. He knew now that he would never understand all there was to know about them and this fact intrigued him. The science lab yielded to his persistence, so did intricate math problems, but women, ah, women would continue to be the eternally unsolved.

Especially when the girls with whom he was involved were two such opposites as Charleen Morgan and Mike Patterson.

Like most males, he had learned very early to divide his life into business and pleasure. He went about his school activities wholly absorbed in them. When he was in the lab, he concentrated upon his scientific experiments and brooked no interruption by thoughts about girls. He tended to business on the basketball court. But there were moments when all work was finished, when there was nothing urgent to occupy his thoughts, and then Mike and Charleen came swiftly in.

In all fairness, he had to admit that it was Mike who came rushing into the vacuum first and Charleen came only as the third party in what had become the most dramatic upheaval in his life.

I am caught, he would say to himself, between the devil and the deep blue sea. Charleen is the devil, let's not kid ourselves. Mike is the deep blue sea, unfathomable, subject to storms and squalls, with a powerful undertow that could catch hold of a guy and pull him on and on, out to sea.

I could go overboard for that girl, he told himself. Completely overboard and for good.

The trouble was Mike did not know it and he knew she would never believe this, even if he had told her. Not after what had happened at the Valentine Dance.

Now that had been a sad business. He did not see himself, as Mike saw him, a boy who had become attached to one girl, a girl in his own class if you will, and then had willfully led on another girl with whom he could never become serious.

Jeff saw himself as a victim of circumstances. The circumstances were miserable ones, he admitted, but they were not of his choosing or planning. Charleen had catapulted herself into his life long before Mike had. Catapulted was the only word for it. She had seen him last spring getting his boat out of drydock at the country club and she had sauntered over to talk to him. He had found her attractive. She did all the things he liked to do, sail, swim, play tennis, ride, dance, and she did them well.

She tugged at his sympathy. She was not a happy girl. She had troubles at home. Her mother's second marriage had been to a man with whom Charleen was always at sword's point. Her eyes were frequently red from weeping when he picked her up for a date. It was hard not to want to put your arm around her and kiss her and tell her please to stop crying, that you couldn't stand to see a girl cry. It was gratifying when she smiled through her tears and forced herself to be gay for his sake.

He enjoyed being seen with her at first because she was

glamorous, a flamboyant creature who drew the eyes of every other boy and envious glances from many girls.

She could be full of fun when she wanted to be.

All this was to the good.

Then, gradually, much too late to save himself in time, he realized what was happening. Charleen was weaving her web around him. Before he knew it, he was inescapably caught, or so it seemed to him.

Now she was demanding and possessive. Time and again he planned how he might break from the network in which he was caught. He would assert his freedom. He would have a day of reckoning with Charleen. He would say to her: See here, this has gone far enough. We're not engaged, you know. You can't monopolize me like this. I've got to have other friends. We're much too young to be serious about each other. Besides, I don't think you and I would really make a go of it, Charleen. You're flighty and capricious. I think in time you'd get just as tired of me as I am of you.

Besides, I don't like to be chased. I want to do my own chasing.

But he had never said any of these things to Charleen. He didn't know how to begin. So he had grown used to waiting for the bright moment when she would tire of him, as she had done of other boys before him, and take to chasing someone else.

That moment had never come.

Instead, Mike Patterson had come along and he had found in Mike all the things he had hoped for in a girl. Mike was no baby, as Charleen was emotionally. She was sensible, sincere, genuine. She was not as dramatic as Charleen, not so attractive to the vast majority of males, and this was something that pleased Jeff. He had had enough flamboyance to last him a lifetime.

He had tried to play it straight with Mike. He never meant to treat her as his "second girl," someone he dated whenever he could get away from Charleen.

The trouble was that he couldn't have played it straight, no matter how much he wanted to. Charleen would not permit it. She was there, in all her surface charm, smiling at him and saying quietly to herself, If you think you're going to toss me aside for that basketball-heaving amazon, you've got another guess coming. Why, she isn't even pretty. How can you want to date her, Jeff? She hasn't half as much to offer you as I have.

So he was caught. He had known it even before the basketball game in which Charleen had embarrassed him out of all countenance by that public demonstration of affection. He had known it long before the dance at the Longshore Club when he had wanted to be with Mike, had wanted to dance only with her and tell her even more plainly how much she meant to him.

He had known it, but of what use was the awareness of such a fact when Mike did not know it. Mike did not understand. She was angry with him. Every time he telephoned her, he felt the ice in her voice.

She would never see him again. He didn't blame her. That was a dreadful thing Charleen had done to Mike. He would have enjoyed slapping Charleen across her beautiful face for what she had said. He had not slapped Charleen. He had lectured her, at length, but that was long afterward, when they were alone in his mother's car. Charleen had burst into tears, but Jeff had not put his arm around her in sympathy. He had sat aloof, angry and upset.

Charleen had forgiven him and begun chasing him again in two days, but Mike had not forgiven him.

She would never forgive him. He was convinced of that. This bothered him. He wanted to see her, to talk with her, just to be with her again. He missed her. He could not stop missing her. Once, during a busy day at school, he found himself thinking about her not once or twice but a half dozen times.

This is awful, he said to himself. This is crazy. I can't go to her because she won't even talk to me over the telephone. I can't just walk into her house because she'd probably order me to get out. I can't see her and I want to see her. The more I try to forget her, the more I find out that I can't.

THIRTEEN

THE BRAMPTON-WESTBROOK game was to be the big one of the year, the decisive event in which the tournament cup would go to the school that won.

It would be played at Westbrook on a Thursday evening and tickets were snatched up almost as soon as homeroom leaders held them in their hands. The students were as eager to see what would happen when Mike Patterson and Emma Gaudet got out there on the basketball court as they were to see Westbrook beat Brampton.

Of late, it had been obvious to everyone that Miss Yates rarely sent Mike and Emma on the court at the same time. Rumor had it that Mike and Emma could not play through a whole game together without tearing each other's hair out. Emma would be sure to start it, and Mike Patterson was never one to run away from a fight.

The very hope of such a showdown in the final game drew the crowd out. It would be fun to watch the fur fly. Fly it would, everyone was sure. You couldn't play a final tournament game and not keep your best guard and your best forward in throughout most of the game. In minor games, against teams that did not measure up to Brampton's playing stature, that was feasible. Westbrook substitutes were going in and out all the time. Not so in the forthcoming game. Mike and Emma would be in there and they would be in to stay.

In addition to the feud between the guards and the forwards, there was the prospect of another dramatic row among the cheerleaders. Add to this the fact that Brampton was a formidable rival, with a team composed of tall, fast players—they were called "The Jackrabbits" in scholastic circles—and you had a game that promised to be a humdinger.

For everyone except the players. Mike approached the final combat warily, with more caution than zest. She knew Brampton. She knew Emma Gaudet. She knew the Westbrook cheerleaders and their widespread unrest. She knew herself and her distaste for the kind of basketball she would have to play, tense, aggressive, under the spotlight of popularity, with the stands full of spectators whistling and howling their lungs out.

It would take steel-edged nerves to stick with the game. She was depending on her experience and natural ability to help her survive the pressure.

She felt less confident about some of her teammates. Shirl Scofield's nerves were raw. She had come perilously near cracking in a minor game last week. Deedie Camp was an impulsive player. The substitute forwards, Mary Melillo and Boots Overton, were still an untried pair as far as a tournament scrap was concerned. Pixie Dunn was a veteran but erratic, excellent one day, a dud the next.

Lynn Craig was Westbrook's best substitute forward. As the season progressed, she had developed into a good player. Mike knew that Lynn had a terrific eye for the basket. She could sink almost any kind of shot, hook, chest, pivot, crip, jump, one-hand push, overhead, set, shoulder, underhand loop. Lynn had learned them all, some better than others. For versatility, she eclipsed Mike. But Mike had observed another trait of Lynn's game. Throw out the smallest thing to disturb her, and she forgot she was playing basketball. Just like that. In the time it takes to hurl a ball from the center circle to the nearest player, Lynn could be transformed from the best basket shooter Mike had ever seen to a crazy greenhorn making every shot a "hope shot," a wild desperate lunge that hadn't a chance to score.

She plays with her emotions instead of her head, Mike thought, watching Lynn in practice games. It's a shame too. She'd be an unbeatable player if she could only learn to take things in her stride.

But it seemed as if Lynn would never learn. All season Miss Yates who was equally well aware of Lynn's strong points and weaknesses had been trying to re-educate this potential star athlete away from her emotional approach to sports.

Mike thought a lot about Lynn and she reached one conclusion. There's something deep and fundamental bothering that girl, she reasoned. None of us has struck the trouble yet. No amount of talk will do Lynn any good, not unless she opens up and tells us what's troubling her.

At first Mike had thought it was merely the stage fright that attacks most freshmen when they first play in a varsity game. However, as the season progressed and Lynn's shooting improved but her mental attitude did not, Mike suspected that something more · than stage fright was wrong with this girl whom she found otherwise so likable.

The night before the big game, Mike broke her own training rules to keep a date with Red Goodrich. There was little use in trying to study. When Red called and asked if she'd like to go over to the Mill Pond for their last skating date of the season, she accepted.

"Do you good," he told her. "I know how it is before a final game. You just sit around and wait. Only makes you nervous. Like a racehorse who gets too jumpy before the race."

Red had his sister's car and they drove out to the pond. It was spring now, the last week in March, but evidently the weatherman had not been let in on the secret, because it was cold and the pond was frozen solid. The old Mill Pond made an ideal place to skate. The townspeople had rigged up giant floodlights that played upon the ice. A concessionaire sold coffee and hot dogs. Some of the skaters had brought along a record player and amplifier so there was music in the air.

The evening and the setting were sheer magic and Mike could not help having a wonderful time. She and Red skated alone. They practiced fancy figures. They tried dancing together on their skates. Then they joined a lively group and played snap-the-whip.

Finally Red reminded Mike that she was playing a tournament game tomorrow and they ought not to stay too late. "I'm responsible for bringing you here tonight," he said. "I don't want to be responsible for getting you over-tired."

So they reluctantly tore themselves away from the gay crowd. On the way home they stopped at their favorite diner for milk and a sandwich. Red was more fun to-night than he had ever been. Now that he was used to Mike, all the bashfulness was gone.

When he pulled into the Patterson driveway he hopped out, and for a few moments he and Mike chatted softly inside the old-fashioned storm vestibule of the house.

"Play a good game tomorrow," Red said. "I'll be right there, Mike, rooting the loudest for you."

"Thanks."

Suddenly Red reached out and caught her to him. "Mike, I think I'm in love." The suddenness of his act and words was such a surprise that she tried to pull back, but Red held her fast. "Mike, will it be all right if I kiss you?"

"No, please don't. I mean, it would be all right but you'd better not."

Red almost threw her away from him. "What kind of double talk is that? It would be all right but I'd better not do it. That kind of language doesn't reach me."

"I mean that if you do, one of us will be sorry. One of us will be hurt."

"No, what you mean is," and every word had a sting, as if Red were slapping her with every syllable he uttered, "you're still carrying the torch for Jeff Parker. You don't want anyone else to touch you. You ought to see how silly that is, Mike."

"I think you'd better not try to poke into something that's none of your business, Red." She was angry too.

"This is my business. You're my business, Mike. I love you. Look, those aren't just words tossed off care-lessly because we've had a wonderful evening together. This isn't easy for me to tell you, Mike. But you mean a

112

lot to me. I don't want to see you throwing yourself away."

"I told you not to meddle, Red. If I throw myself away, that's my business."

He grabbed her again, but not in affection. He pulled her around so she had to look at him.

"Mike, that's a silly thing to say. You use words the way you toss around a basketball. Words aren't that easy to handle. You've got to be more careful of them. No matter what you say it is my concern if you do something to yourself that's going to make you miserable."

"Red, let go of me. You're just hurt because I said you shouldn't kiss me."

"I'll let go of you. But first I'm going to have my say. I'm not hurt on account of a kiss I didn't get. If I want a kiss, I can get one from some girl who likes me a little more." She tried to pull away, but he held her, making her face him.

"Mike, I've been watching you for weeks. You're not the same girl you were the night I took you to the dance at Longshore. You've changed. That night you were a wonderful girl. Direct, honest to a fault, but I liked that fault. You appreciated me and that made me feel comfortable. More even than that, I liked being with you because you had an air of fun about you, as if it was good just to be alive. You cared about other people, too. You were the most genuine person I'd ever met."

"But now I'm not. I've changed. I'm different," she said defiantly. "You just said so."

"Yes, you are different. You've done something to yourself, and I'm not sure I like it. You've put on a lot of glamour but that's not all. You've been trying to change things deep inside you. Trying to be blasé, just a little bored with life and people."

"I had fun tonight. Did I act bored on the pond?"

"You never do when you forget your new sophisticated pose," Red flared back.

"My pose!"

"Yes, your pose," he insisted. "Because that's what it is. You've been spending the last month practicing a part. Trying to be the girl you think Jeff Parker will fall in love with. It won't work, Mike. Things like that— phony things—never work."

"I must be a pretty terrible person," she said huffily. "Blasé. Posing all the time. A phony. I don't see why you bother with me."

"Because I love you, Mike. Remember? I told you so five minutes ago. I love you because I don't for one minute think you'll ever succeed in this act you're putting on. You can try it out, but you'll always be Mike Patterson. The real Mike Patterson I met the night of the dance. She's a pretty swell girl. Take it from the guy who loves her."

He let go, this time for good. He turned and left, flinging the storm door wide open and running and slipping across the snow to where his car waited in the driveway.

Mike stood there long after Red had pulled out. She closed the door and fell back against the wall of the vestibule, putting her hands over her face, thinking.

All the things Red had said to her whirled in her mind. She could not put them out. They seemed to catch the rhythm of one of the songs to which she and Red had just danced on the Mill Pond.

Mike, you've changed. You were the most genuine person I'd ever met. You've done something to yourself and I'm not sure I like it. Trying to be the girl you think Jeff Parker will fall in love with. It won't work, Mike. Things like that—phony things—never work. You can try it out, but you'll always be Mike Patterson. She's a pretty swell girl. Take it from the guy who loves her.

The words were caught up in the melody of that song which she could not chase from her mind. Round and round they went to the music. She clapped her hands over her ears to stop them, but they would not stop. They danced in her thoughts, leaving her bewildered and frightened because she could see that in his anger Red had told her the truth.

FOURTEEN

THE NIGHT of the Brampton-Westbrook game got off to a bad start. When Mike and Pat ran out to the car, the battery was dead. It would take at least an hour to get any service station to bring out a booster battery. Pat's frantic telephone calls to friends revealed the fact that everyone had already left for the game. Mike and Pat finally took a taxi and their parents arranged to drive in later with neighbors.

Mike was silent on the ride to the school. Late already, she was fretting about time. Miss Yates had told them to be there by six-forty-five. It was seven o'clock.

When the taxi swung into the parking lot, Mike jumped out, leaving Pat to pay the driver. Mike ran across the lot, calling terse greetings to the people she passed. At last she reached the dressing room and found it almost empty. One girl was still dawdling at the far end, but Mike was in too much of a hurry to pay any attention. She snatched her basketball suit and sneakers and started to undress.

As she was getting into her uniform, someone called her name. Shoving her head through the opening in her shirt, Mike saw that it was Lynn Craig.

"Hi," she said shortly. "You still here?"

"Yes. I stayed because I want to talk to you, Mike."

"*Talk!* It's pretty late for chit-chat, Lynn."

"This isn't chit-chat. It's important."

Mike wanted to brush Lynn aside, but something in her expression told Mike that what Lynn had to say couldn't wait.

"All right," she said. "Let's have it." She didn't mean to sound so abrupt, but she was annoyed with Lynn for

115

picking the night of the big game for a heart-to-heart talk.

"I couldn't tell this to anyone but you, Mike." Lynn stammered the words. "You, you sort of understand me."

Mike's thoughts screamed, Spill it, and let's get out of here! But she merely nodded for Lynn to go on.

"Please ask Miss Yates not to put me in the game tonight," Lynn pleaded.

"She probably won't have to put you in," Mike replied. "Shirl and Deedie are here. We've got Pixie Dunn in a pinch. Boots and Mary are fairly good subs." She thought, Honey, you're at the bottom of the pile. Don't kid yourself. Miss Yates thinks you're too much of a risk. She'll only use you in an extreme emergency.

Lynn was persistent. "I've got a feeling she's going to put me in. A sort of intuition. It's a big game and anything can happen, Mike."

"True enough."

"I don't want to play tonight. I can't."

Mike looked quizzically into the face before her. "Why not?" she asked.

"Because my whole family will be here."

"So what?" Mike shrugged. "All our families will be here. My father will be there in the front row bellowing his head off. My mother too."

"They'll be cheering you, Mike. But my family is different."

"How?"

"They don't like me."

"That's silly talk."

There were tears in Lynn's eyes. "It's true. You don't know. No one knows about my family. I'm the baby and a girl. I've got five older brothers. They don't think I can do anything. They tease me all the time. They told me they were coming tonight just to razz me." The tears came in earnest now, rolling down Lynn's freckled cheeks. "You haven't any idea what it's like. Your family loves you. You all stick together. Pat even got into a fight with the cheerleaders to help you out, Mike. My family isn't like that. Not about me. I'm something to make fun of.

116

It's always been that way. They," she sobbed out the words, "they just don't care anything about me."

So, it's out at last, Mike thought. This has been the trouble all along. She had known it must be something fundamental to foul up Lynn's basketball game the way it did. Her inferiority complex was so deep-seated that Mike had felt it must spring from some pretty big frustration.

Mike's quick sympathy was roused. Her feelings reached out toward the girl in front of her. Life was stern enough without being nagged by the notion that your own family was against you. She saw the whole picture. A sensitive girl brought up in a family of tormenting brothers. The teasing had probably started long ago in fun, but things like that could get out of hand, they could become habitual and nasty. Mike felt for Lynn, even more because her own family relationships were so satisfactory.

Mike's impulse was to throw an arm around Lynn and comfort her. Yet her common sense told her that would be the worst kind of sympathy to offer.

"I think you've built this family stuff up, Lynn, far bigger than it really is," she said. "Besides, it's possible your brothers were only joking about tonight. They may not even show up."

"Yes, they will!" Lynn flared back. "They're here already. I saw them in the gym. All five of them, sitting in the front row, with bags of popcorn in their hands."

Mike pictured five tall boys, sandy-haired and freckled like Lynn, sitting in the front row and holding five bags of popcorn in front of them. She squelched the impulse to smile.

"Personally, I don't see why you should be called in to play," she said. "We've got a complete second string of forwards without you."

"Then you won't speak to Miss Yates about it?" Lynn's voice was taut.

"I'm sorry, Lynn," Mike spoke quietly. "I can't. It would seem to be telling Miss Yates her business. I think we'd just better wait and see what happens."

Lynn ran from the locker room. Mike wanted to call,

"Lynn, wait! Don't take it so hard. I'm on your side. I do understand, but can't you see that if I ask Miss Yates to keep you out of this game it will make a quitter of you all your life?" But instead Mike stood there, her hands clenched at her sides, saying nothing.

The locker room was quiet now. Mike felt a heaviness settle down on her, a deep foreboding of trouble ahead. She felt her responsibility as acting captain in a way she never had before. She saw things bigger tonight. In this moment of decision, faced as she was by this problem of Lynn Craig, she saw what it meant to be a leader. People not only looked up to you. They brought you their woes and heartaches. You figuratively held their hearts and their lives in your hands as you said, I will do thus and so, or I will not do thus and so.

Bowed by the weight of this thought, she turned and walked slowly toward the gym.

When Brampton ran on the court in their orange and black uniforms, Mike's uneasiness settled into heavy gloom. They looked huge! "The Jackrabbits" they were called and that's exactly what they resembled, towering dark jackrabbits with legs and arms flying in all directions. They had the stance, the swagger, the toothy smiles of a team that had come out here to win.

The gym was packed to capacity. It was bedlam. Crowds of students still milled in, searching for seats, shouting to friends, crawling over the adults in the stands with muttered apologies. The Brampton cheerleaders attempted to outshout the Westbrook cheerleaders who in turn attempted to outscream everyone.

Mike was not one to let her eyes wander from the metal rim of the basket to the stands. Yet tonight, as she warmed up, running toward the basket and rolling the ball over the rim, her glance was drawn toward the spectators. She found her parents easily. They sat where they always did, first row near the officials' table. Flash Feeney was conspicuous in his yellow scarf and battered hat, shouting his greeting to Mike. Red Goodrich was not difficult to find either. His hair was a beacon, about halfway up on the Westbrook side. It pleased her that,

118

in spite of their near-quarrel of the night before, he had come out as he promised. He waved to her reassuringly as she glanced in his direction.

Jeff was not so easy to locate. She knew he would surely be there because he had telephoned her this evening during supper, to say he would be looking for her.

"I want to see you after the game, Mike," he had said.

"Maybe," was the most encouragement she would give him. To herself, she admitted that she had good reason to want to see him too. This afternoon she had decided that she must return his silver skier to him. The decision was not so sudden as it appeared. For weeks, ever since the V.I.P. dance, she had been thinking about it. Several times she had been on the point of wrapping it up and sending it back. She knew she had no right to keep it. The sentiment that had prompted Jeff's giving it had long since dissipated. Then the talk with Red last night had decided the issue for her. Red was right. She was playing a losing game. She could never be the kind of girl Jeff wanted. Everything was against it. The background and the money she didn't have. But even more than material things, her own nature was against it. Red had told it to her straight. *You'll always be Mike Patterson.*

In a deeper sense, she felt that what Red had been saying to her was, You'll always be the "My Sister Mike" Emma Gaudet has dubbed you. You can't be truly beautiful, the alluring kind of girl Pat or Charleen Morgan is. You might as well settle for what you are. Plain-Jane Mike Patterson. A good sport. A good egg. A right guy. But not the kind of girl Jeff Parker could ever be devoted to. He would always want another girl, the glamorous kind of girl, somewhere in the offing. This, in essence, was what Red had said to her. And it hurt. She rebelled inwardly against it, even while she accepted it for what Red believed it to be, gospel truth. Red said he loved her, and yet with his love he was putting upon her the stigma of limitation. He was binding her all her life to what she did not want to be, a second fiddle, a light-weight. "Take a back seat," Red, who professed to love

119

her, was virtually saying, "you're just somebody's 'Sister Mike.' "

These thoughts raced through her mind as she ran again and again toward the basket and laid up her shots. She played like an automaton, putting the ball in almost every time, but her mind was perplexed and harassed. She felt pulled apart. She wanted to clap her hands over her ears to shut out the bedlam in the gym. She wanted to scream at the top of her lungs, "Stop it! Let me alone! Everyone let me alone!"

Mike snapped out of the preoccupation to see that the referee was beckoning to her to join the Brampton captain. Mrs. Tolles was official for tonight, a tall, blond young woman a few years out of college. Mike liked her.

She talked to Mike and the other captain, a girl whom Mrs. Tolles called "Jean," dark-haired, bronzed, and swift of eye. Mrs. Tolles was brief in her instructions. Then she sent them back for the starting whistle.

Brampton received the ball in the center circle. Their forward turned, paused, looked, then sent the ball heaving over the heads of the Westbrook guards to their towering forward near the basket. It was the old Brampton game of basket-hanging and Mike groaned as she watched it work as effectively as it had in that early game of the season. The giant near the basket stepped aside from Emma who was guarding her for a pivot-shot and the ball went in. The Brampton stands went wild.

Mike watched Emma Gaudet bite her lip as she walked away from the basket. The play had been so swift, so neatly planned and executed that Emma had not even been able to get into the act. Westbrook rooters were screaming their displeasure. "Whassamatter, Gaudet? Where were ya? Why didn't you stop that ball?"

Emma's face was scarlet. She could hand it out, but she couldn't take much of this punishment.

Shirl Scofield went into the center circle for Westbrook. Westbrook was tipped off on the play to follow. Mike would receive the ball from Shirl. That would bring both Mike's and Shirl's guards to the side. Then Shirl would dart down the center toward the basket to be there in time to catch the final pass and toss it in.

Mrs. Tolles tossed Shirl the ball. She caught it, pivoted, held it lightly between her fingers as she scanned the Westbrook side. Deedie was clapping her hands for the ball to draw attention from Mike. Shirl passed to Mike who caught the ball easily. She turned to send it to Shirl. Shirl's guard bounced around her like an elongated rubber ball. It rattled Shirl, but she tried to dart away to recieve the pass. The ball zoomed at her and Mike noticed Shirl's shakiness. Shirl got the ball but she fumbled it. It bounced from her and the Brampton guard pounced on it. It went back into Brampton territory. Emma Gaudet lunged for it. She sent the ball back to Westbrook. Mike made a dash for it. But Shirl was nearer. Again Shirl missed and the ball went hurtling back to Brampton. This time one of the Brampton forward's caught it, turned, dribbled, and sent it spinning toward the basket-hanger. Emma jumped for it and missed. The forward caught it and spooned it neatly into the basket.

Brampton, 4; Westbrook, 0.

The Brampton stands went wild again, but even above their cheers Mike could hear the Westbrook protests.

"Hey, Gaudet, get in there. This is a basketball game, not a golf tournament. You got lead in your arms? Whassamatter with you? Need glasses or something, Gaudet?"

Mike watched Emma. She appeared to pay no attention to the heckling, but her mouth was a tight line. Mike called for time out and huddled her team in a circle at the side. Before she had a chance to speak, Emma lit into her.

"If you're going to preach a sermon," she snorted, "save your breath. I'm doing the best I can guarding a super-woman half a head taller."

"I'm not preaching," Mike started to say, "but. . . ."

Emma cut in. "You forwards stick to your own knitting. We guards will stick to ours."

Mike leveled a glance with Emma. "Why do we have

121

to let a bunch of jackrabbits scare us? All they've got is height."

"And speed," Deedie spoke up. "They're plenty fast."

"What we need," Emma sneered, "is some brains."

"This time you're right," Mike agreed. "If we had brains and used them, we wouldn't be scared."

"Who's scared?" Emma leered around at her teammates. "I'm not scared, I'm mad!"

"That doesn't help either," Mike said quietly.

"Preaching," Emma muttered. "Always high and mighty preaching. Come down out of your pulpit, Sister Mike." Mike drew back from the taunt.

The referee's whistle broke up this cozy little tête-à-tête and Mike went back to her position with Emma's vindictive sneer ringing in her ears. *Sister Mike, Sister Mike, Sister Mike!* The walls seemed to catch the hateful nickname and fling it back at Mike, bouncing the words around her ears. The time out which Mike had intended to use to strengthen her team had only served to split them into factions. For one dreadful moment, Mike churned with anger and hatred for Emma.

I can't reach her, she thought. We're farther apart than we ever were.

There was no time for nursing this kind of thinking because the game was on again and it went along like greased lightning. Fast, hard, rough. It was a game that never let up. Brampton played terrific basketball. They were a team inspired. They had come out to win.

The score at the end of the first quarter was Brampton, fifteen; Westbrook, four. Mike had managed to hook two of them from center court before the Jackrabbits descended on her.

During the two-minute quarter break, Mike lay on her back on the floor, listening to the cheers from both sides. The Westbrook cheers sounded half-hearted. She could understand why. So far her team had hardly covered themselves with glory. But even worse to endure than the lukewarm cheers was Emma's muttering. She lay near Mike tossing out gems of sarcasm, most of them directed toward "My Sister Mike." No one answered her.

That made it even more pointed. The strain between the Westbrook teammates was unbearable. Mike wanted to scream, to shout out and hear her own voice reverberate in the big gymnasium. She didn't know what she wanted to shout, she just wanted to scream anything to drown out the echoing of Emma's voice with its bitter tirade against "My Sister Mike."

The quarter break was soon over and Mike jumped up to go back into the game. Physically she felt rested, but her thoughts were in a turmoil from Emma's browbeating. She just couldn't keep her mind on the game.

The second quarter was not much better than the first. Westbrook held Brampton down a little. The score at the half was twenty-three to fourteen in favor of Brampton. Mike felt Westbrook's five goals had cost them too much. Four of them had been made by Shirl Scofield, but Shirl cracked up on her final basket. She made an overhead shot that strained her arms and sent her sprawling on the floor. Mike was the first to reach her. She saw what the real trouble was. Shirl was shaking, sobbing hysterically. Her nerves had snapped. Mike had seen it coming on for days. Now it happened. Shirl went out and Pixie Dunn came in.

It was a real bad break. Next to Mike, Shirl was the best basket-maker on the Westbrook team.

Mike decided to spend the long intermission alone. She ran down the hall toward the deserted physical-education office, avoiding the crowds in the corridors. Miss Yates knew where she was going and had given permission. Mike needed this time alone. To think. The pace of this game had been so fast that she felt exhausted from the sheer impact of Brampton's strength.

One thing was clear. Westbrook was not going to beat Brampton by brawn alone. Brampton had it all over them. They were big, powerful girls who could get in there and stay in there.

On the other hand, Mike's team was a bundle of nerves. Everyone was jittery. Everyone was fed up, worn out from the strain of a season that had started so well and was threatening to end in total disaster for Westbrook.

Mike looked down at her hands. They were trembling. She didn't show it outwardly so much as the other girls, but her own nerves were frazzled too.

She began with herself, calming down, arguing herself into some semblance of control. It didn't take too long. She had disciplined herself for years to take the hurdles of life in her stride and now this self-discipline was paying off. She began to relax. She found her poise.

Then she started to think.

First she took rapid stock of the game. Twenty-three to fourteen. At the half Westbrook was nine points behind. Not an irreparable situation, but a pretty serious one. A fresh, dynamic team with lots of spirit might make up the difference and forge ahead to win.

But Mike's team was not a fresh, dynamic one. Shirl Scofield had just been yanked out on an injury bad enough to keep her out of the rest of the game. Pixie Dunn had gone in for her. Pixie had played varsity basketball for years. She didn't have a nerve in her body. She didn't have any zing either. She played a routine, uninspired game, sometimes better, sometimes worse, but never tops. Perhaps Miss Yates was giving Pixie a chance to see if this was one of her better times. If not, she'd be pulled out fast.

Let's face it, Mike thought. We begin the second half nine points lagging, with a weak offensive.

Now let's look at the defensive.

The Westbrook guards were a fast, efficient bunch. There was only one thing wrong with them. They were dominated by Emma Gaudet. Mike thought briefly about Emma. She was a lot of things and none of them very good. She was clever, but she knew it too well. She was a clown. She could be malicious. She could be hard and cold, and she was drawn tightly into a shell which Mike had never been able to penetrate.

That was too bad. Because in Emma lay the key to the only chance Westbrook had to win.

From her position as forward, Mike had noticed something. She doubted that anyone else had observed it, not even Emma herself. Most of the girls played with their minds on their own game. They seldom paid much attention to what was happening to anyone else. Mike doubted that Miss Yates had noticed it because you had to be in there, right in the thick of the game, to see it happening.

The Brampton forward whom Emma was guarding was, like Mike, a specialist in one kind of shot. Where Mike's was a hook, this lanky bean pole had developed a terrific pivot shot. A pivot shot was a wonderful help to a tall player. If you towered above your guard the way this girl towered above Emma, you simply stepped aside, moving on a pivot, then you tossed in the ball. That's all there was to it.

It was a lot easier than hooking them from way out in center court. You almost never missed. Like most easy things, it had its disadvantages. If someone was smart enough to study your pivot, analyze your stance, your private little quirks, that someone could learn how to guard your shot.

Mike had, almost unconsciously, been studying that basket-hanger from Brampton. She had been given plenty of opportunity to do this. The towering forward had made ten of Brampton's goals.

In short, Brampton was playing a one-girl game. Cripple this girl's game, and you crippled Brampton.

Mike knew how to do it. It would take a fast, smart guard, one who was quick on her feet, nimble and adroit. A tricky player. Emma Gaudet was all of that. If Mike could get to Emma, could tell her what she herself had observed, they might stop Brampton yet.

Only Mike had never yet been able to get to Emma.

Mike considered talking it over with Miss Yates. The coach would be in the dressing room, speaking to the girls about the game. Never the kind of teacher who believed in a corny pep talk which went in one ear and out the other, Miss Yates used the individual method of approach. It worked too. She had, under normal conditions, the best organized team in the county. This year, everything had gone haywire, but it wasn't Miss Yates's fault.

Mike took a couple of steps toward the door, intending to find Miss Yates and talk to her. She stopped short.

That was not such a good idea.

Miss Yates would be surrounded by girls. It would be impossible to talk with her privately. The tight little clique of guards stuck together. One of them would notice Mike talking with Miss Yates and manage to overhear the conversation. If Emma found out that Mike had been the source of instructions issued by Miss Yates, she would ignore them.

Mike stood there undecided, wrenched this way and that.

Why don't you go to Emma yourself?

The question crept quietly into Mike's mind. She brushed it scornfully aside. That would do about as much good as whamming a basketball into a concrete wall. The basketball would make no dent in the concrete. Mike would make no dent in Emma.

An insistent argument set up in Mike's mind. She stood apart, listening to it with fascinated detachment, wanting nothing to do with it. Yet it went on.

Look, this isn't just yourself that's involved. Your precious pride which might be smashed by a few remarks from Emma's sarcastic tongue. This is something pretty big you're facing. It's not even just a matter of winning a basketball tournament. That's pretty important but there's something bigger than that.

This is the whole world right here in the palm of your hand. This is what's wrong with everything, with everyone wherever there is anything wrong. People hating people. Not just whole vast hordes of people hating other vast hordes of people. But just one little guy or gal hating another little guy or gal.

Sure you hate Emma. Don't kid yourself. You don't like her, do you? You don't trust her. Well, there aren't two ways with love or hate. It's one or the other. You think she's mean, petty, vicious, back-biting, capable of doing or saying almost anything. You think she's hopeless. You've given her up. No matter how thin you slice it, it's enmity. Bitter, entrenched enmity.

No, I will *not* go to her. I will not help the girl who dubbed me "My Sister Mike!" *It's war, Mike. It's all there is to war.*

The argument within her plunged on, relentless, unyielding.

You're afraid of Emma because you hate her. Hate and fear. The same thing. No difference. We hate what we fear. We fear what we hate.

You could go to her. You could talk to her. No, don't shake your head. Don't be so *afraid* of her. She's only what you are, nothing more, nothing less. When you go to her without fear, she'll listen to you. She'll have to listen.

The voice within was insistent now, no longer pleading, no longer arguing. It came as a command.

Go to Emma, Mike. It's the only thing to do. Go and talk to her yourself. Don't *try* to talk to her. Go with the determination to *do* it.

Mike recoiled from the insistence within her. For a moment she stood there trembling on the brink of indecision. Then she put her shoulder against the door and shoved it open.

She ran down the hall to the dressing room. Maybe it was too late. The halls were clearing. The intermission was almost over. She ran, pushed on by a compelling force within. At the door of the dressing room, she paused. Then swung it wide. The place was still full of girls getting ready to go up to the gym. Her eyes sought the tight huddle of guards. No Emma.

She backed out and ran along the corridor, blindly, not knowing where to find Emma. She searched every crowd she passed. She turned and looked at every girl in basketball uniform. No Emma.

She found her just outside the entrance to the gym talking to a couple of boys. Mike touched her arm and Emma wheeled around. For a moment both girls faced each other, neither speaking.

"I want to talk to you alone," Mike said firmly.

Emma looked at the two boys. They were staring at

Emma and Mike with interest. Emma hesitated. Then she spoke to the boys. "I'll see you later."

She stepped out of the gym and followed where Mike led her to the turn in the hall. Mike stepped back into the shelter of a doorway and beckoned to Emma.

"What's this all about?" was Emma's surly question.

Mike took a breath so deep that the air pressed hard against her lungs. Her throat was dry, her mouth feverish. When she spoke, the words caught in her throat and she had to force them out.

"That forward you're guarding has one shot."

Emma sneered. "You brought me out here to tell me what any six-year-old can see?"

Mike ignored the sarcasm. "A pivot shot isn't the toughest kind to guard."

"You try it sometime," Emma snorted. "Against a six-foot-two giant."

Mike watched how she fed her information to Emma. It had to be done just right or it wouldn't hit the mark. She mustn't let Emma think she was trying to boss her.

"That bean pole pivots to the right, mind you, always to the right, then dribbles and makes her lay-up shot from the right." Emma didn't answer, but she was lapping up what Mike said.

"That Brampton forward can't shoot if she is forced to the left," Mike went on. "She hasn't got enough balance to pivot to the left and she can't make her lay-up shot from that position. She's missed only two shots. Both times when you forced her to the left." Mike was thinking, *accidentally* forced her, but she omitted the telling adverb.

Still Emma didn't speak.

"I was thinking"—and now Mike talked fast because time was running out—"if that Brampton giant was constantly crowded to the left after she received the ball by your stepping forward on your left foot, she couldn't pivot to the right. When she pivots to the left, cut to the basket, guard her shot, and recover the ball. We might just win this game yet."

Emma didn't move. She didn't bat an eyelash, but her

128

expression told Mike all she wanted to know. Emma had her cue. She knew what to do.

She asked Mike just one question before they ran down the hall to the gym.

"Why did you tell me this?"

Mike grinned slowly.

"I'm a sucker for liking to win."

There was a flicker of a smile in Emma's eyes. Her facial muscles didn't move. No smile came, but she did manage to squeeze out a "thanks" as she ran ahead of Mike down the hall.

The gym was, if possible, even noiser than at the start of the game. Mike went to her place on the Westbrook side. This time she did not scan the stands for friends and relatives. She had only one thing on her mind now. *Lick Brampton!*

Brampton's forward stood in the center circle to receive the ball from Mrs. Tolles. She caught it easily, holding it just a second to glance over the court, then she sent it hurtling toward the forward nearest her. She ran back, zig-zagging through Brampton territory, evading the Westbrook guard, catching the ball as it was sent again to her. She turned and tossed it toward the basket-hanger.

Mike, near the center on Westbrook's side, watched. Emma was poised. She had the perfect control of a natural athlete. There was no indication that anything was different from what it had been during the first two periods. Only Mike, a veteran player herself, could detect that there was something different. It showed in Emma's stance, in the taut line of her jaw, in the tilt of her head. She was ready.

As the ball hit the hands of the Brampton bean pole, Emma moved in, crowding her from the right. She had to toss the ball to someone else or make a try for the basket. She chose the latter. She pivoted to the left, lost her balance, made a weak stab at a lay-up. The ball hit the rim, teetered, hung in the balance, and bounced off.

Westbrook rooters rose to a man and howled their delight. "Attza stuff, Gaudet. That's showing them. Keep it up!"

Emma paid no attention. She caught the ball, recovering with the agility of a big cat, and sent it hurtling back into Westbrook territory. Mike was there to catch the pass. She turned, saw Pixie clapping her hands for the ball, but decided not to let her have it. There was no time to lose. They had to make baskets. Make them fast and make them accurately.

Mike hefted the ball in her right hand, aimed for a shot. There was one thing about a hook shot. It was the most difficult shot in the whole repertory to guard. She took her aim, paused a second, then let it go. It went straight for the basket, a clean shot from almost dead center of the court.

Brampton, 23; Westbrook, 16.

Westbrook screamed their cheers. The place was pandemonium. Mike hardly heard. She cut toward the center line, hoping Emma would send her the ball again.

Emma did. She did it again and again. The game took on a new rhythm. Mrs. Tolles to Brampton center forward, center to the forward at the line, forward to bean pole basket-hanger, Emma moving swiftly in to kill the shot, then a wildfire recovery by Emma, ball zooming through the air to Mike, Mike turning, pausing, taking her time on her shot, a clean one straight for the basket.

At the end of the third quarter, the score was tied. Brampton, 26; Westbrook, 26.

Mike had made six baskets with her famous hook shot. Brampton had made one goal as one of their forwards, not the basket-hanger, had darted in for a clean chest shot. The other Brampton point had been made on a free throw when Deedie Camp had piled up her third personal foul of the game.

During the rest period, the circle of Westbrook players huddled together on the gym floor was surprisingly quiet. No one had anything to say. Not even Emma who lay flat on her stomach, face down, breathing hard. She had played a terrific game of basketball and Mike would have enjoyed telling her so.

Near the end of the break, Miss Yates sent Boots Overton on the floor to replace Pixie Dunn. Mike breathed more easily. Pixie was no good tonight. Erratic as always, she was completely off her game. Boots was green, but at least she could handle a basketball.

When the whistle called them back into the game, Mike noticed that Brampton had switched the positions of its guards. The girl who had been guarding Deedie Camp had swapped places with Mike's guard.

It soon became clear why the change had been made. On the first play, Mike saw she was being crowded away from her post in center floor where she usually elected to receive a pass. Back, back, her new guard crowded her, forcing her to dart around the floor for an opening, covering her with an uncanny understanding of Mike's game. Mike got no chance at the ball.

Mike could almost hear the Brampton coach giving the instructions which this new guard had apparently received. "You can't guard a hook shot, but you can keep her from getting the ball. *Keep Patterson away from that ball.*"

The shooting switched to Debbie and Boots. That was too bad. Deedie, always impulsive, ran up a technical foul in the first minute of play. Brampton booed Deedie who looked pretty well shaken. Mike watched Miss Yates as she walked over to the scorer's table to check on Deedie's fouls. The coach decided to take her out. She turned and beckoned to her girls on the benches.

Mike hardly paid attention. Mary Melillo would come in. It was the logical thing to expect. It wouldn't be good, but Mike would have to make the best of it. If she could shake off the leech who was guarding her, she might run up a few baskets herself. Mary and Boots were good for a couple apiece. With Emma holding the fort over in Brampton territory, Westbrook had more than a fair chance to win.

It would mean hard work, not letting up for one second, but it would be possible.

Then Mike saw something that almost made her eyes pop. It wasn't Mary Melillo who was reporting to the officials to enter the game. It was Lynn Craig.

Mike didn't have time to figure out what was back of

131

Miss Yates's move. The game was on and she was in it. And a tough game it was.

Brampton had changed their offensive as well as defensive. They no longer depended on their basket-hanger to do all the shooting for them. A new forward had come in to replace one of the girls who had been feeding the ball to the basket hanger. She was small and wiry, a human dynamo who bounced all over the floor after the ball. Among the tall jackrabbits of the Brampton team, this half-pint stood out in stark, dramatic relief. She won the admiration of the stands as she darted for the ball, then ducked in toward the basket with a short dribble and used a jump shot to put it in.

She ran up four goals, a total of eight points before Westbrook had even caught their breath.

By a switch of tactics from zone to man-to-man defense Westbrook guards finally managed to stop her spectacular march on the basket.

But her work had been done. Eight points was no mean advantage in the third quarter, especially with a crippled Westbrook offensive on the court. Mike ruefully contemplated Westbrook's prospects. She was handicapped by her leechlike guard. Boots was adequate but just that. Lynn Craig stood there with a scared expression on her face. She looked as if she would burst out bawling if someone so much as pointed a finger at her.

Mike was grim. She watched Boots go to the center circle to receive the ball. It would take a miracle to save Westbrook now. The game which had looked fairly easy a few minutes ago was slipping from their fingers.

If she could only get that ball for a hook shot. If she could only get free of her guard!

Then the miracle happened. It was one of those little things that don't seem to amount to much at the time, but it turned the trick.

The ball went from Boots to Lynn. Lynn stood there, staring at it. Mike, exasperated, let out a shout that pierced the noise and hubbub in the gym.

"Shoot, Lynn!" she screamed. "Don't be chicken-hearted. Shoot!"

Lynn wheeled. The stands, sensing tension on the court, quieted down. Into the silence that sliced across the big place, Mike screamed again.

"Shoot, Lynn! Don't be chicken. Shoot!"

Lynn's face twisted with hurt, but only for a second. The hurt gave way to surprise, then determination. She wheeled, took her stance for a shoulder shot, and sent the ball toward the basket. There was more than mere skill in her shot. There was anger, hurt, shock. Mike had startled her into shooting and she gave it everything she had. The ball went neatly into the basket.

Brampton, 34; Westbrook, 28.

The Westbrook stands led by Pat Patterson cheered the freshman who had made the goal.

"Craig!" they bellowed. "Do it again, Craig!"

Lynn glanced over at Mike as she walked back to her place. Mike could not tell much from her expression. She seemed a little unsteady. Mike, in the aftermath, was somewhat appalled at what she had done. She had shouted at Lynn without thinking, because there was nothing else to do but shout.

Except for that quick exchange of glances, nothing passed between Mike and Lynn. The game was on again. It settled into the tense, furious pace of the final minutes. If Westbrook was going to win, they had to make some goals fast.

Mike, standing there as the ball went to Brampton in the center circle, watched her guard. She was tiring. These last minutes showed up a player's weaknesses. Mike's guard had been playing the game to the hilt and the task of keeping the ball from Mike during the third quarter had been an exhausting one.

This was the moment Mike was waiting for. Now she might get her hands on the ball again.

She did. It came to her on Emma's first recovery of the ball in Brampton territory. Mike wheeled. She could try for a hook shot and she might make it. The guard jumped and darted in front of her, trying to stop the shot, expecting that Mike would do the inevitable, take her chance at the basket.

Mike fooled her. She saw Lynn within easy tossing distance of the basket and she sent it to her. It was a long chance. The kid's first shot might have been a lucky fluke. Sure, she was a dead shot at the basket in practice games. Out here, Mike wasn't sure. She didn't know whether the kid could do it again. But she sent her the ball.

She saw it hit Lynn's hands. Almost felt the sting of it herself as it bounced into Lynn's open palms. Lynn wheeled, pivoted, and sent a perfect crib shot into the basket.

Brampton, 34; Westbrook, 30.

The place was crazy with noise. Mike registered the ear-splitting screams like someone in a dream. She felt lifted up out of the gym, to a world where all that existed was Emma Gaudet, Lynn Craig, Mike, a basketball, and a metal rim with some knotted rope hanging from it.

The ball came at her again. Again she stepped aside from her guard and caught it and again she sent it to Lynn. Lynn caught it, hard, jumping for it like a seasoned player. She wheeled and sank an underhand loop shot.

Brampton, 34; Westbrook, 32.

Once again Mike shut out the roar around her. She watched the ball pass back and forth from one side to another as Brampton fought hard to keep possession and shoot. They did but the shot went wild, a "hope shot" that fell short of its mark.

The ball came to Mike and again she let Lynn have it. The kid's eyes were shining. All the fear was gone. The hurt, the anger were washed from her face. A half smile curled her mouth. Her cheeks were flushed. She jumped for it, turned, and sent in a one-hand push shot.

Brampton 34; Westbrook, 34.

Mike glanced at the scoreboard and at the same moment she heard someone shout, "Look at the clock!"

She did. The second hand was just past the halfway mark. There was one minute and a half to play.

Brampton took the ball in the center circle. It went to their tiny forward waiting at the center line. Then she made the fatal mistake of the game. Instead of darting toward the basket herself, she seemed afraid to take the chance. She sent it to the basket-hanger. Emma was there, crowding the tall girl toward the left. The shot missed. Emma recovered and sent it over to Mike.

Mike turned. She could hook it in. There wasn't a doubt in her mind that she could. This was her moment of decision. She held the game literally in the palms of her hands.

Then her eyes went to Lynn, flushed, shining, with a glow of triumph over her.

Mike thought, this moment belongs to her.

So she made up her mind. Like that, in the twinkling of an eye, in no longer than it would have taken her to send her own hook shot straight for the basket. She let Lynn have it.

The kid caught it on the run, racing to meet it. She turned with the screams of all Westbrook deafening her ears. She paused only a moment, then she let it go. It banked against the backboard, teetered, then dropped through the metal rim for a goal.

Brampton, 34; Westbrook, 36.

The buzzer sounded. The game was over.

Mike pushed through the crowd that milled out upon the court. The place went wild, but she managed somehow to get to Lynn. Lynn was standing in a charmed circle of her own, surrounded by five proud brothers. Lynn's face was still flushed.

They looked at each other, the tall dark-haired girl with the grin, the sandy-haired one with the stars in her eyes.

"You did all right, greenhorn," Mike said.

"Thanks," the kid answered her. "Thanks for everything."

FIFTEEN

THE DRESSING room was almost empty now. Mike had taken her shower and she was dressed in a new camel-colored suit. She stood before the mirror and combed her hair carefully. Then reached for a red scarf and tied it at her throat. A bit of lipstick, a touch of powder, and she would be ready. She wanted to look her best.

In the mirror, she saw the gleam of the silver skier as it dangled at her wrist. Jeff would be outside the dressing-room door waiting for her. Red would certainly be there too. And Flash. Her parents had caught her on the way out of the gym to say they were going on home with the friends who had brought them. Pat had gone off on a date. Mike had told her family not to worry. She'd surely get a lift.

Mike smiled. How things had changed from the days when she was family chauffeur! Her thoughts wandered back to that day a few short months ago when she had been here alone thinking about Jeff Parker. That day she had almost collapsed when she swung open the door and found him standing there. She remembered herself as she had been that day, nervous, loquacious, without a speck of poise. Jeff had seemed so wonderful and inaccessible. She had been unpopular. A girl so unwanted that the V.I.P. Club made her the target for an initiation joke.

Everything was changed. Jeff was no longer a remote creature. He was the boy with whom she had fallen in love and for a time she believed he had returned that affection. She was no longer unpopular. She was someone to be reckoned with, a V.I.P. in her own right. No one would make her the target of a joke now.

It had cost her something. The events that had brought her popular esteem, had brought also disillusionment and some suffering.

So tonight her problem was different from the one that day when she had swung open the door to face a worried, if resolute, Jeff Parker.

When she pushed open that door five minutes from now, there would be three boys at least waiting for her. She would have to decide what to do about them and she hadn't the cockeyedest notion what that would be. Flash had become almost her "steady" and everyone called her his "girl." Red was her best friend. She admired him, leaned on him, turned to him with her troubles. Jeff she still loved. No mistake about it. She could fight it off, stifle it, squelch it, argue herself black and blue about it. Jeff was still the boy of her choice.

She dawdled over her make-up, figuring out what to do. It occurred to her to suggest that the three boys take her to the Greasy Spoon for a sandwich. For a few seconds she enjoyed the thought of herself flanked by three adoring males. Then she abandoned it completely. Before the evening was out, someone was sure to have punched someone else's nose.

She thought of having three dates, in rapid succession, first with Flash, then Red, then Jeff. She imagined herself racing over to the Greasy Spoon with Flash, then transferring to Red's car for a snack at the bean wagon, and finally she pictured herself and Jeff in the foyer of the Patterson house saying good night. She gave up this idea as impractical because of the time element involved. The vision of an irate Mr. Patterson standing at the head of the stairs and shouting to Jeff that three o'clock was an outrageous hour to be bringing his daughter Mike home settled the matter.

She would have to choose one of the boys and as tactfully as possible eliminate the others.

It was at this point that the door swung open and Boots Overton came running over. Boots was out of breath.

"Mike," she ran her words togther, "I've-got-a-message-for-you. You're-wanted-in-the-girls'-physical-ed-office-at-once."

"What for?" Mike asked. The game was over. Westbrook had won the tournament. Mike's conduct had been irreproachable. What on earth would Miss Yates want to talk with her about?

"What does she want me for?" she asked Boots again.

Boots was in a terrific hurry. "I-don't-know," she said. "I-don't-know-anything-about-anything. I-just-know-that-I-was-told-to-tell-you-to-go-to-the-office."

Mike growled to herself as Boots ran out. A moment before she had faced the not unpleasant dilemma of what to do with three boys. It had been baffling but altogether entertaining. To have her party spoiled by a summons to Miss Yates's office was a distinct anticlimax. She glanced over at the door outside which she was certain her three boys waited. Then she reluctantly picked up her coat, bag, and mittens and walked in the opposite direction towards the girls' physical-education office.

She opened the door and looked toward Miss Yates's desk. Her chair was empty. Then she became aware of another presence in the room, but not Miss Yates. She turned toward the opposite side and looked into the face of a smiling Jeff Parker.

Quickly she put the pieces of the puzzle together.

"You sent that message to me!"

"Yes," he said affably. "There was too much competition."

"Do you think it was honorable to say Miss Yates wanted to see me?"

"I didn't say that," he replied. "The exact message was, 'Tell Mike Patterson she's wanted in the girls' physical-ed office at once.' "

Mike conceded the point. "I naturally thought it was Miss Yates."

"I'm sorry if I've made you mad."

"I'm not mad," she said. "I didn't have any real dates with Red and Flash, and I did sort of promise you. Besides I didn't know how to handle the situation. It snowballed on me." She was thoughtful. "We ought to send

138

them some kind of message. It's not right just to walk off."

"I've thought of that, too," he said. "In five minutes, after we've gone out the back door Boots Overton is going to tell them that you've left."

"Boots is quite a friend of yours," Mike said.

"Not Boots. Her two brothers. I'm teaching them to ski."

"You're a very ingenious guy, Jeff Parker," Mike said.

"You don't know the half of it."

Mike stared at him and he stared back and then they both burst out laughing.

They drove over to Jeff's house. He said that was the only place in the whole country tonight where he could have Mike to himself. "Every restaurant and dog wagon and hamburger heaven for five miles around will be crowded." And Mike agreed.

They went in the back way, into the kitchen. They sat at the snack bar and ate the sandwiches and cake and drank the chocolate milk Webbsie had fixed for them.

Then they went into the game room and turned on the record player, softly so as not to disturb the rest of the house, and they danced in their stocking feet.

It was the most fun Mike had had since the last time she had been in this house and danced with Jeff in this very room.

At last it was time for her to go and she told Jeff so firmly, refusing all his pleas to stay longer.

It was while they were in the kitchen getting on their coats that Jeff mentioned Charleen. He brought up the subject himself.

"I don't quite know how to talk about this, Mike, but I'm terribly sorry about what Charleen said at Longshore."

"That was long ago. Things that happen so far off ought to be forgotten."

"But I want you to know how I felt."

"I think I know, Jeff."

"Do you, Mike?" He came toward her, but she turned away. "I wouldn't blame you if you thought I was a fool.

I have been foolish where Charleen is concerned. It's hard to explain. I don't want to make myself a hero and make Charleen seem like a brat."

"Jeff, I've got to tell you why it's so important to me that we be very sure about Charleen. About you and Charleen."

"I think I know, Mike."

"No, Jeff. You couldn't know. Not really, not unless you were Mike Patterson. I've got to tell you about Mike Patterson, Jeff. She was a tall, lanky, not very pretty girl when you met her. All her life she'd been living under a cloud. In the shadow of a beautiful and popular sister. She was just *'My Sister Mike'* to the crowd at school. She didn't hate her sister, or even envy her. But Mike Patterson sometimes got very angry at herself. She wanted to be beautiful and adored too, just like Pat. Then one day she met a boy whom she liked very much. She thought she had a chance with him. But there was another girl in the picture. Her name was Charleen and she was glamorous. She was everything Mike Patterson wasn't, and the boy seemed to like this other girl. In fact, he seemed bound to her with unbreakable ties. So Mike Patterson tried to change herself. She tried to be glamorous too. And sophisticated and very poised and very attractive."

"Mike, listen. . . ." He tried to interrupt but she cut him off.

"No, Jeff, I've got to finish. This is the most important part of all. This girl, this Mike Patterson we're talking about, knew another boy. A boy named Red. One night he told her that she was all wrong to try to change herself, that she'd never succeed, that we all had to be true to what we really were. We shouldn't try to be something artificial. If we wanted to be happy, we had to stick to being our true selves."

"Red had no business talking to you like that."

"Yes, he did, Jeff. He's my friend." She would not tell him that Red had declared his love. "My very good friend. He told me this last night. He wants me to be happy. I can never be happy being a phony, Jeff. I've got to be myself. That's why I've got to be sure you like me as I am. Plain-Jane Mike Patterson."

"You're not plain-Jane to me, Mike. You're the most wonderful girl in the world."

He walked over to where his cap and mittens lay on a stool and picked them up. He stood with his back to Mike. She thought he would never turn around again. When he did, the embarrassment between them was gone.

"You're right, Mike," he said. "I had that coming to me." He came quickly over. "There won't be any more Charleens." He smiled. "I've had a bellyfull."

"But what can you do?" she asked him. "She'll never let you alone."

"Remember back at the school you called me a very ingenious guy?" She nodded. "I've got a cousin. You don't know him because he goes to Hotchkiss. He comes home every weekend. Two weeks ago I introduced him to Charleen. He's six-feet-two, has black curly hair, black eyes, the kind of face girls fall for. Hard. Charleen took one look at him and made up her mind."

"Did you introduce them on purpose?" Mike inquired ever so casually, but her throat was tight and dry. Whatever Jeff answered to that question would be the turning point for both of them.

"Just as much on purpose as I sent Boots Overton after you tonight," he said. "You see I figured it this way. My cousin—Gregory Watkins is his name—Greg's a chaser himself. He gives a girl an awful rush and then he gets tired of her. He and Charleen have a lot in common. I figured they might do each other some good." He looked into Mike's eyes.

Then he fished in his pocket and brought out a box. He placed it in her hand and she opened it.

"Why, it's another silver skier!" she exclaimed.

"A girl," he prompted her. He touched the other. "This one's a boy skier. I thought he ought to have some company. Steady company."

She clutched the skier in her fist and smiled up at him. "This wouldn't be another part of your V.I.P. assignment, would it?"

"No. Because I now belong to another club. The P.I.V. Club."

"I never heard of any P.I.V. Club."

"Pretty Important Victory." Their laughs rang out.

"Sssh!" Mike cautioned. "We'll wake up your people. Someone may come down."

"Don't care if they do." Jeff took her in his arms, but before he kissed her he said, "They might as well get used to seeing me kiss my one and only."